fascination

fascination

a novella

KIM BROWN

ONE

Timmy spied her again. There was a pang in his chest as she walked into the classroom. He was in the habit of getting to this class a little early just so he could see her come in. He watched her as she turned and sat a couple of rows in front of him, his eyes glued to her beautiful bottom in skin-tight jeans.

He had fantasized about her many times. She was so beautiful. He would lay in his bed at night imagining her coarse dark hair that reached most of the way down her back. He could see her face, visualizing every detail: her wide-set dark brown eyes with thick eyebrows arching above, her high cheekbones, her full beautiful lips with slight dimples on either side of her mouth. Her face had great structure and proportion. It drew him in and made him want to stare. Then he would picture her beautiful body in his mind. She had firm, medium-sized breasts with an upright shape. He could only imagine what they looked like without clothing or what her nipples looked like. But the long curve of her hips and the shape of her derriere were right there for him to see when she wore jeans or tights. The way it protruded, the crease on either side at the cusp of her ass where it met her legs, and everything about the size and shape of it turned him on. Everything about her turned him on; everything about the way she looked.

Her name was Annette, but he didn't even know that much. He had never spoken to her.

On this day in class he had decided that he was going to ask her out on a date. He had never dated anyone when he'd been in high school. Now that he was in college, he was still shy, and beautiful girls made him extremely nervous. He was so attracted to them, looking from afar, wanting to be sexually involved, fantasizing about different girls that he had seen. But he had no clue how to approach them, what to say, or how to get involved.

He already had his books in his knapsack ready to go when class ended. A wave of dread washed over him as he sprang out of his seat and caught up to her near the front of the class. He hesitated for just a beat, and when he started to speak, she gave him a vague smile, turned, and walked away.

*

"Annette."

She heard a silky, deep voice call from a short distance down the hall as she stepped out of the classroom.

"Hi, Luke," she answered in a sultry tone.

She had met him just the other day at a college café there on campus. And he had remembered her name.

Her mind snapped back to that occasion remembering the first words she'd overheard as he was talking to a friend of his shortly before they met, "Now, she's a classy girl. I love what she's wearing. I love her style."

She looked at him now as he walked toward her. He was cute. He was clean-shaven, and there was a curly strand of his jet-black hair hanging on his forehead between a pair of sparkling blue eyes. He had a strong jaw and a beautifully shaped mouth. She was dying to kiss the two tips of his top lip. He wasn't extremely muscular, but he had a great-looking chest and a flat stomach that was well revealed in the tight pullover shirt he was wearing. None of this was conscious thought. It all came in a moment from someplace inside, someplace beyond her volition.

He had a relaxed smile and, without hesitation, lightly placed his hand on her hip as he spoke, "I'm so glad I ran into you."

"I meant to give you my number the other day when we met," she replied, "but I had a class to run off to."

"Yeah, it's crazy how busy this college life can be. Hey, I don't mean to keep you if you've got someplace you need to be."

"No, actually, I don't have another class until later this afternoon."

He had released his hand but was standing close, in her

space. She loved the way he smelled, not like cologne. It was more subtle. It was his scent.

"Great," he responded with that beautiful deep voice.

"Do you live here on campus?" she inquired.

"Yes, actually, very close by. Would you like to come over?"

She reached around his back and draped her arm lightly around his waist as they began walking together down the hall.

It was an automated dance: the dance of two people who had been immediately, viscerally attracted to each other.

*

"Hey, dude! Get out of the way." The voice came from another student as he was tapping on Timmy's shoulder trying to get out of the classroom.

Timmy absentmindedly shuffled out of the doorway to let the other students pass as he stood there with his mouth agape, watching the interplay between Annette and Luke. They were on their way to enjoy what he had only dreamed about.

TWO

She was a beautiful young woman. She knew it and used it to great advantage for her own pleasure. If you were an interested young man who didn't capture her attention, she would ignore you or dismiss you with a glance. She could also decide on someone and not let on until she knew she could have him.

Annette was a longhaired brunette. She was tall, but not too tall. Her shape was very attractive and she looked great in tight jeans. She looked great in just about everything. Perhaps she looked best in nothing at all.

Annette was a college student in her sophomore year. She had been doing well, but college was not her primary interest. College life outside of the classroom was.

She had been sexually active in high school but kept it on the down low. She never wanted to have a reputation or have to put up with all the high school bullshit that went along with having an active sex life. She confined her sexual involvement to older guys, mainly college guys, and people who weren't part of that whole high school grapevine. The fact that she never dated any of the guys in her high school had its negative ramifications, too. She was thought of as one of the "stuck up chicks" by some and as an "eternal virgin" by others. But at least she was never labeled a slut. That word had never crossed her mind.

Annette was selective. She could be. And she learned the hard way that she needed to be. Her radar was well developed. She really hated that one time when she'd made love to a guy and then he got all "I love you" on her. She hated to be mean to guys, and she wasn't trying to break anybody's heart, but she had no interest in getting tangled up in a relationship at this point in her life. She was enjoying her life just fine without it. Ordinarily, she never had an ongoing sexual relationship with a guy. It was just too risky. Once in a while, if a guy was really good and she felt confident that he wasn't going to get all smarmy and demanding, then there'd be a second time. Third times didn't happen.

There was a time during her first year at college when she was seeing a particular guy that she liked. He took his time and was man enough to take her cues. She could talk to him as they were making love. He got to know what she liked and how to do it. And she enjoyed turning him on. The more turned on he got, the more turned on she got. It was a beautiful cyclic event. They shared some great lengthy sessions, keeping each other on the brink. Not to mention some glorious, intense orgasms. She was making love to him on a pretty regular basis for a couple of months. But then he wanted to do the exclusive thing and started making noise about her being his girlfriend. She had no interest in being anybody's girlfriend.

One evening after making love, he whispered in her ear, "I'm loving being with you. I'd really like to keep this between you and me. You know?"

Annette looked at him quizzically, and he added, "You know, boyfriend and girlfriend? I mean, I'd rather just be involved with you."

She kissed him on the cheek and replied, "That's sweet, but I'm not ready to settle into an exclusive relationship."

She got up and started getting dressed. "Hey, I've got to go," she said. "I'll talk to you soon."

He watched her leave with a forlorn look on his face.

A day later, he called her on the phone and asked, "Hey, Annette, have you given us any more thought?"

She stammered, "Well, uh, like I said, I don't think I'm ready for that."

Now, with a tinge of angst in his voice, he shot back, "Oh, c'mon baby, we're crazy about each other."

She wasn't sure how to respond but said, "Look, I love being with you, too, but I'm not ready."

She hung up.

He immediately called back, now with anger in his voice and said, "This is crazy; don't you get it? We should be together, otherwise we should just break it off!"

"Okay. I think that would be best."

She hung up again.

A couple of days later, he called again. "Hey, Annette,

I'm sorry. I won't pressure you anymore, but I'd like to keep seeing you."

Silence on the other end.

He finally spoke again and said, "Hey, what are you doing this Saturday?"

After a brief pause, she responded, "I'm going to be busy. Please don't call again," and she ended the call.

Unfortunately, the calls and drama kept coming, so she ended up changing her cell phone number. An extreme hassle.

There were those times when she had other not-so-pleasant experiences due to her sexual appetite, or maybe it was because she was a good-looking girl who didn't necessarily want to entertain every Tom, Dick, and Harry's bullshit just because they wanted to try and get involved with her. She was out one evening on the weekend at a college bar, The Applegate, that she usually enjoyed and had good luck at. But she finally left that particular bar on that particular evening because there was a particular guy that was a particular pain in the ass and just wouldn't leave her alone. So she was off to a new venue on her quest for a significant rendezvous with a non-significant other.

She thought about it later and wondered, *Why did I have to leave because of him? I should have just called Tom, the bouncer.*

Well, sure enough, about two weeks later she ran into this same guy on Friday night. She noticed him out of the corner of her eye but never looked at him, never got near him, never even walked in his direction. But before long, there he was in her face, trying to come on to her, trying to be all sincere while checking her out and generally making her feel very creepy. She tried to get the guy to leave her alone, but it just wasn't working. She finally stood up and walked over to Tom, who was in his usual spot on a barstool between the front door and the bar. He recognized her. He was always friendly the times she'd been in before, and they'd always had a comfortable and pleasant repartee. Tom had his own thing. There wasn't any girl good-looking enough to get his attention when he was at his post at that bar. Women were just not on his agenda at that time. Tom was a very large black man of few words. He was just big and probably stood about six foot five or something. The other thing about Tom was that he was paying attention. He had a good eye on pretty much everybody and everything that was going on in that bar. So when she walked up in front of him, no words were exchanged. All she had to do was nod her head in the direction of the guy that was sitting at the table she'd just left. Tom stood up and slowly walked over to the table. Then he folded his arms across his chest. Very large arms and a massive chest. He just stood there and looked at the guy. At first, she felt kind of bad for the poor guy, yet at the same time, she was amused. Tom didn't speak. After staring at the guy, who was looking back up at him, Tom finally rolled his eyes, turned his head toward the door, and then looked back down at him. The guy was still sitting there trying to act casual.

There was another guy sitting at a nearby table with his girlfriend and he muttered, "I think it's time for you to leave."

Finally, Tom said in a very calm voice, "There's been a complaint."

The guy was still sitting there looking up at Tom. "What are you talking about?"

But before he could finish, Tom said, "Dude! Are you listening? If I have to tell you again, I'm gonna pick your skinny ass up and throw you out that door!"

With that, the guy stood up. "You don't have to be rude," he said as he scurried toward the door.

Annette made sure she was facing the other way when he went by. She returned to her table and whispered "Thanks" as Tom went back to his usual post.

At that point, she'd pretty much lost her focus when a couple of her girlfriends came in and sat down with her. They ordered a round of drinks. There happened to be a particular band there that night that she'd heard before and really liked. There was something about one singer's voice that captivated her. So they spent the evening together, and Annette was content being with her friends and listening to the music.

She wondered later on whether Tom ever actually used all that beef of his or whether his stature alone was enough to settle any arguments. She asked him about it on a later occasion.

He smiled. "Well, the deck is pretty well stacked. I'm a martial arts practitioner, and I make it a point to stay in practice. And I teach martial arts when I'm not here."

"Are you a black belt?"

"Second Dan," he replied. "Not to mention all of the bar managers have permits for concealed weapons, so there's always somebody who's carrying. Plus, I've always got my cell phone. I can dial nine-one-one without looking. Nine-one-one is our preferred method of treatment when things start to get out of hand. But we can usually keep the wolves at bay till the blue lights get here."

She finished her chat with Tom and got back to her focus of finding the next date.

THREE

She hadn't met him until that night, which was often the case. He was good-looking with thick, short cropped blond hair. She hadn't even noticed him before he made the first move, which was unusual. But before she knew it, they were laughing and had shared several enticing tactile moments. His hand lingered on her shoulder, which she encouraged by lightly placing her hand on top of his. A little later, smiling and chatting, he placed his hand on her hip. She leaned in closer to him, laying her hand on his forearm. It had a firm athletic feel as she lightly stroked the fine covering of blond hair.

Before too much longer, she decided it was time to get their interaction to another level.

"Well, I think I need to be going," she said while still fondling his arm.

"Oh, I'm sorry," he responded. "Where are you off to?"

"Someplace with you before we get arrested for lewd behavior."

His eyes lit up and he grabbed her by the hand. They arrived at her place, which was close by, and before he knew it, she had him where she wanted him.

He was sitting on the edge of the bed with his pants down to his ankles. Annette was on the floor between his legs with her knees on a pillow. She was naked except for a black thong. She kissed the tip of his penis, which was already hard, then closed her eyes and placed her tongue right into the opening and reached up with her left hand to cradle his balls. These were the moments she loved so much. She opened her mouth and pushed it over his dick, taking the head in. She then reached down with her right hand and began stimulating her clitoris with light pressure in a small circular motion. She licked the underside of his dick, right there where she knew it felt best, and looked up at him, trying to pay close attention and gauge his level of excitement. She didn't want him to come too soon. Then she took her left hand, closed her eyes, and pressed his dick against her cheek while she continued to stimulate herself. The feeling was intoxicating. She wasn't doing any of this just to get him off. It was all about the dick. She was in her sexual glory.

What was it about dick? What was it about a man's penis that turned her on so much? She loved it when it was soft. She loved it even more when it was hard. She loved to make it get hard and then to control the man's feelings and pleasure with it. She loved the sight of it, the smell of it, the feel of it, and especially to have it in her mouth. When a man would undress, she would be so thrilled to watch him take his pants down and to see his pubic hair—the prelude. And then to see his dick.

Invariably she'd get wet during those moments. She even loved to put the dick in her mouth after they'd finished, after he'd come and his dick was soft. There were times when she got herself off doing this and had great orgasms.

Shortly after they'd finished, he got up. Never looking her in the eye, he said enthusiastically, "That was so great." He was hurriedly putting his clothes on. "I'll call ya tomorrow."

He was so antsy, but she didn't mind. She preferred that to the other extreme. She smiled as he left, not revealing her thoughts. *Why did he have to say that?* She knew he would never call. He didn't even have her phone number. It was a good date.

FOUR

Annette's childhood was pleasant if not fairly uneventful. Her mom and dad were both successful people—not rich but they provided a nice home in an upper middle-class neighborhood, and they were close to their daughter. She was an only child with nothing too dramatic in the recollection of her early years.

She got very good grades, and one of her favorite classes during high school was chorus. Through this she had learned the basics of reading music, but mostly she just enjoyed singing and was in several of the choral groups. She'd always sung along with the radio and enjoyed many different styles of music. Her mom and dad were an influence, too, since they often had different types of music playing on the stereo system at home. She heard everything from Louis Armstrong to The Beatles, to Miles Davis and Stevie Wonder, just to name a few.

Annette was a pleasant young girl who got along well with her parents and was eager to help out. On one occasion Annette's mother called up to her from the bottom of the stairs. "Hey, Annette?"

"Yeah, Mom."

"Would you check on the clothes in the dryer?"

"Sure, Mom."

"Oh, and would you check the litter box, too, while you're at it?"

"Sure, Mom."

Not only did she check on the laundry, she folded it neatly and put it away. When she was done with that, she checked on the cat's litter box there in the laundry room. She cleaned that up and added fresh cat litter. Then she went back to work on her homework.

*

Flossie Baker was a longtime friend of Annette's family who lived next door. She was an elderly woman with auburn hair and strands of gray that she usually kept pulled back in a bun. She had deep lines in her face and pale, faded blue eyes, but there was still a certain twinkle whenever she smiled. She was a fiercely independent woman who kept the home that her three children had grown up in even though they had all moved out of town. She was still there several years after her husband passed, but she stayed active and kept the house neat and clean. She had helped out with some babysitting from time to time when Annette was young and loved nothing more than to come over and spend the evening with Annette when her parents were out. However, the first time that Mrs. Baker came over to babysit, Annette was a little disappointed.

Annette's mom told her, "Hey, Annette. Your dad and I are going out tonight, but we won't be late."

"Oh great!" she replied. "Is Heather coming over again?"

"No, sweetie. Heather can't make it tonight. Our neighbor, Mrs. Baker, is coming."

"Mrs. Baker? But she's too old."

"Annette Brennan, watch your mouth. You be respectful. She's a very nice lady, and she was glad to help out."

"Okay," Annette said as she lowered her head slightly.

Mrs. Baker arrived later that evening at the appointed time, and Mrs. Brennan showed her around the house and gave her a card with both her and Mr. Brennan's cell phone numbers on it.

"Just call anytime if you have any problems or any questions." Her parents stepped out.

The next thing Annette did was turn on her mom and dad's stereo system in the living room. She had left Mrs. Baker in another room while she found her favorite radio station and then turned the volume up. She turned it up just loud enough, so she thought, that Mrs. Baker wouldn't approve.

Flossie Baker immediately walked into the room, looked at Annette, snapped her fingers and said, "Turn that thing up. I really like that one."

Annette just looked at her in disbelief, walked back over to the stereo, and twisted the volume knob. Sure enough, Flossie Baker was singing along as she took off her coat and hung it up in the hall closet.

Annette was also soon to discover that Flossie Baker was quite a storyteller. She was a wellspring of anecdotes garnered from a lifetime of experiences. Annette would sit wide-eyed as Mrs. Baker told stories about her own youth, about people she knew, and the many escapades that her own children had survived.

From time to time Mrs. Baker would spy Annette after she got off the school bus and invite her in for a snack.

"Don't tell your mom I'm feeding you this stuff. She wouldn't approve. It's really not good for you, but don't it taste great?"

And they would both enjoy eating something that Annette would usually never get at home.

On one particular Saturday, Annette was looking forward to getting out with some of her friends. Annette's mom was going to be driving them to the movies, but later that afternoon Annette saw the swirling red lights of an ambulance in front of the house next door. She ran downstairs to tell her mom. Her mom asked Annette to wait there and ran out the front door to see what was happening. When she came back, she relayed the bad news to Annette. Mrs. Baker had fallen and was being taken to the hospital.

"Are we going to the hospital, Mom?"

"Well, not tonight, dear. I've got some things to take care of after I drop you and your friends off at the movies."

"But isn't she going to be all alone?"

"Well, you know I don't think she has any relatives close by. Maybe we should."

So, Annette and her mom canceled their plans, got in the car, and drove to the hospital. Mrs. Baker was alone in her room when they arrived. They could see a look of despair on the old woman's face when they first entered, but she instantly lit up when she saw Annette. Fortunately, her injury was not that severe and she was able to return home the next day.

When Annette got older and started singing with the choir at school, Mrs. Baker made a point to be there whenever there was a performance. Theirs was a relationship that they both enjoyed through the years, and Mrs. Baker would be the one person that Annette sometimes confided in as she experienced her teenage years.

Annette had started to express her interest in the opposite sex, telling Mrs. Baker about some of the boys she knew at school. One afternoon after Annette got home from school, they were enjoying one of their clandestine snacks together when Flossie started in on one of her stories.

"You know," Mrs. Baker said, "my daughter dated a couple of young men when she was in high school. She was all excited about this one fella that she thought was so good-lookin'. But when she told me his name, I recognized it. He had already graduated. Anyway, I said to Claire, 'Ain't he engaged?' and Claire says, 'Yeah, but they're breakin' it off.' So, I said, 'Well, I just read about the engagement in the paper. Who told you they were breakin' it off?'"

"So, then what happened?" Annette questioned as she sat there with rapt attention.

"Well, Claire said that *he* said they were breakin' it off. And I said, 'Umm hmm? And how's his fiancé gonna feel when she finds out?'" Flossie Baker sat there stroking her chin, looking into Annette's face just the way she had looked at her daughter years ago.

"So then what happened?"

"Never heard no more about him after that."

*

Annette had been exposed to many pearls of wisdom from the sage old Flossie Baker. But her parents certainly imparted their knowledge and influence on their daughter as well. There was a conversation they had with Annette when she was in her teens. It was "The Talk" about sex. They were actually fairly relaxed about it, mainly encouraging her to be safe. They explained about different contraceptives. They encouraged her to take her time and get involved with someone she had a connection with. They talked about falling in love, but also about being involved with someone who you liked and had things in common with.

"You know, Annette?" her mother said. "You'll find that

sex is the best when it's with someone that you really love. It'll be great when it happens, so don't be in a hurry."

What they didn't know was that she had already been seduced by an older college student and her fascination had already begun.

FIVE

It had happened on a Friday night when Annette was in high school. She was excited to be on her way to her girlfriend Cindy's house for a party. Generally, Annette's mom and dad trusted her, and she had never been one to get in trouble. The party was at Cindy's parents' house on the other side of the neighborhood, so Mom was dropping her off, and Dad had agreed to pick her up later on at 11:00 p.m. What Mom and Dad didn't know was that Cindy's dad was out of town, and Cindy's mom was pretty much down for the count, having picked up the flu. So, the party for Cindy and her friends carried on while Cindy's mom was up in her bedroom on the third floor.

Cindy would turn out to be Annette's best friend in high school. She was the same age but different in many respects. She was almost always cheerful and outgoing. She had strawberry blond hair, a round face with pleasant features, and an impish smile.

The party was a pretty normal event for Annette and her friends, a bunch of high school girls hanging out at one of their parents' homes, listening to music, comparing notes about boys, and talking trash about the girls they didn't like. But then Adam strolled in through the kitchen door. He was with Cindy's older brother, Paul. Annette immediately noticed him, as did the other girls. The fact that he was a little older and in college seemed to put him in another league compared to the boys she knew in high school. But there was something else about him. He wasn't that tall or that great looking, but he was fairly well built, kind of stocky with shoulders and a chest. But the something else had to do with his entrance into the room, his presence. He didn't seem to even notice her or the other girls. There was more of a relaxed confidence he put out that none of the boys her age had. More often than not they were awkward, trying to impress her and always saying something stupid.

Adam was a more experienced young man, having been sexually active for a couple of years with his high school sweetheart. But that relationship had ended about six months ago when she moved out of state for college and he stayed behind attending the local community college.

A little later on, Annette's interest got the better of her. She sat down next to him on the couch, trying to act nonchalant.

"So," she said, "you're at the community college."

"Yeah." He looked at her out of the corner of his eye. Looked at her with a certain crooked smile as if to say, *Well, it's about time you noticed me.* "Hand me that drink," were his next words as he pointed to a can of soda in front of her on the coffee table.

She obliged and, in handing him the can, their fingers touched. He was looking into her eyes at that moment without expression, and that mere touch shot through her. It was the highlight of the night so far.

And so they began to chat over the din of music. Cindy caught her eye from across the room and gave her a wink. But before too long, he excused himself, rose from the couch, and walked out of the room. A few moments later, Annette decided to use the restroom and walked across the room away from the din of the party. But when she tried to open the door to the half bath in the hallway, it was locked. She walked into the bedroom of the guest suite a little farther down the hall. A lamp in the corner on the other side of the bed was dimly lit and the room had a cozy feel. The door to the private bath in the suite was open, so she walked in and used that bathroom. When she came out, she was startled to see someone else coming into the bedroom.

"I'm sorry. I didn't mean to startle you." It was Adam.

"Oh, not at all."

"Mind if I hang out?" he said as he closed the bedroom door.

She was a little taken aback, but at the same time thrilled to be behind closed doors with him.

"Not at all," she said, again trying to be as nonchalant as she could.

He sat down on the edge of the bed and said, "Boy,

Paul and Cindy's folks have got a really nice place here."

"Yeah, they do." She sat down next to him.

Without saying another word, he turned and looked at her with his face close to hers. He just waited, moving his head ever so slightly closer to hers. And then she kissed him. It was a long and exciting moment. She had kissed boys before, but it was nothing like this. Then she felt his tongue and this kiss became a more active prelude. Then his hand was on her shoulder. She lay the back of her hand in his lap. *Oh my God,* she thought. His jeans were bulging as he started to become erect. She was frozen . . . and totally fascinated. She knew what an erection was, but she had never experienced one before. Again, her interest got the better of her. She turned her hand over and began to fondle this bulging mass. He moved his hand from her shoulder and cupped one of her breasts. He squeezed her ever so gently and then began a circular motion with the palm of his hand, rubbing her nipple lightly through the shirt and bra she was wearing. Oh, what a feeling: his hand on her breast as she rubbed his hard dick through his jeans while passionately kissing and exploring each other's mouths. She felt herself getting more excited and her pussy getting wetter by the moment. She never intended or even dreamt that any of this would happen. She felt like she was being swept along, tacitly engaged in this lust and lost in the moment. He stopped kissing her and stood up. He walked over and locked the door to the bedroom. He then turned around, leaned back against the door, and slowly started to unbutton and unzip his jeans as she stared in wide-eyed wonder. She did not protest or try to stop him. He slid his jeans and his underwear about halfway down his thighs and stood there for a moment taking in her expression as she stared at his hard dick, completely exposed. Next, he reached into one of the pockets of his jeans and held up a small packet. He opened it, and, holding a condom in one hand, put the empty packet back into his jeans pocket. She was mesmerized by the whole activity. He placed the condom onto the head of his hard penis and rolled it down. Now she was dying to have him inside of her. She had fantasized about fucking more than once, popping her own cherry in the process. He kicked his jeans off, then walked over, grasped her shoulders, and they lay down on the bed side by side, facing each other, and began to kiss again. She reached down and grasped his hard dick in her free hand. She loved the feel of it. She just held it and kissed him. Then he began to unbutton her jeans. She kicked her shoes off and wriggled out of her jeans and underwear. He reached around and began feeling her ass with his hand. The touch of his hand on her bare skin there was intoxicating, and she felt herself getting wet again. He rolled her onto her back, she parted her legs, and he positioned himself on top of her with his waist between her legs. He placed the tip of his dick into the entrance of her vagina and waited while they began kissing again. Then he slowly pushed his way in. Now she had her arms around him with her hands on his back as he began to slowly thrust. She moved her pelvis toward him as he pushed in and pulled away slightly as he pulled back, and they began a rhythm. After a few minutes, he started to move faster, and then he pushed his torso up. He was on his hands, at arm's length, looking down at her now as they continued thrusting into each other. He moaned and closed his eyes, coming with his dick deep inside of her. And then the sexual tension was gone from him. He became totally relaxed. They embraced for a moment but were startled by a knock on the door.

"Hey, what's going on in there?" Cindy hollered.

You could hear the sound of the other girls giggling.

"Oh, nothing!" Adam yelled, already up pulling his jeans on.

Annette sprang up, grabbed her jeans, and put them on. She got her shoes on just before he cracked the door open. He was standing behind the door.

He leaned over, pushed his face into the crack of the door opening, and said with a wry smile, "Nothing going on in here."

Cindy looked up at him. "You better not be slobbering all over each other in there," she said as the other girls continued their incessant giggling.

Little did they know.

Adam and Annette walked out of the bedroom. Adam started chatting with Paul, and Annette joined the other girls back in the living room, but for the rest of the evening she had this aching feeling. She had this sexual tension that she couldn't do anything with. The party wound down, and her dad arrived precisely at eleven to pick her up. This night was by no means the beginning of her sexuality. But it was the end of her virginity.

When she got home, she brushed her teeth and went straight to bed. She lay there reeling from the events of the night.

She closed her eyes and at that moment she heard her mom say through her closed bedroom door, "Goodnight, sweetie."

"G'night, Mom."

She then started recounting the evening's events, remembering every detail. She thought about that first kiss with Adam and started to feel herself getting wet. But she did not touch herself. She waited as she was enraptured by her remembrance of it all. She pictured Adam leaning back against the door with his hard dick out. She lay there on her back in the bed, trying to remember exactly what it looked like and then began to touch herself. She cupped her right hand over the mound of her pubic hair and started applying a gentle pressure. Then she gently pressed her middle finger into her pussy, which was now soaking wet, and she began to thrust, just the way she thrusted when Adam fucked her. She kept moving, the aching feeling becoming stronger and stronger as she imagined him inside her, kissing her, thrusting himself into her. Finally, she came—a huge glorious orgasm that seemed to go on and on before it finally subsided. She relaxed, turned onto her side, and drifted off to sleep.

The next morning, she heard a knock on her door. She groaned, rolled over, and looked at her alarm clock, which she had neglected to set the night before. That was very unusual. It was about 7:30.

Her mom yelled, "Better get up. Don't forget, you've got that science study group this morning at nine o'clock."

Annette got out of bed, went into the bathroom, and started getting ready. After a quick breakfast, she and her mom were in the car and on their way over to one of Annette's classmate's house for the study group. Annette's mom stopped the car to drop her off. Annette grabbed her book bag and walked up to the front door. She could hear the sound of her classmates' voices inside. At that moment, Andy walked up behind her. He was another classmate attending the group. He was no one that she was particularly interested in, but he always seemed to perk up when he was around her. Before long they were gathered around the living room, involved in a question and answer process. Andy would call out the question, someone would answer, and then they'd review it to make sure they had the right answer. Annette kept busy taking notes. She was actually pretty good at preparing and wanted to be ready for the test that was coming up the following week. After about an hour they had pretty much covered the material and were wrapping up.

Andy, who was a very good student and had taken it upon himself to lead the study group, spoke to Annette. "Well, looks like you've been pretty studious. I saw you taking a lot of notes."

It was his way of trying to compliment her, but the tone of his voice and his mannerism seemed bogus. He was trying to impress her with some kind of authoritative air. At that moment, the thought of her experience last night with Adam pranced through her mind. She rolled her eyes and never said a word.

SIX

Annette discovered early on as her nubile breasts grew and she progressed through puberty that men of all ages, shapes, and sizes were attracted to her. She picked up on their cues. Some of it was just annoying if not embarrassing, but she pretty readily learned how to derail it. She also learned how to play the game with those she was attracted to. She practiced the art of throwing out the cues: a look, a fleeting touch. She learned how to give the signals without sounding an alarm, and if a guy didn't notice, didn't respond, or was reluctant to engage, then she moved on. She easily moved on because she found plenty of others who knew how to play the game.

It started in earnest after her encounter with Adam. Even though she had not had an orgasm when she relinquished her virginity to him, she was taken. Even though she'd taken herself there afterwards, it wasn't enough. It wasn't the same. The interaction, the uncertain anticipation, the sight, the smell, the touch, and the feeling were compelling her. It became her subconscious mission. It was her dope.

It wasn't too much longer before she scored. It was her

first love-making session, and not some hasty fuck while hoping that they wouldn't be caught in the act.

*

It was a Saturday morning at the local grocery store. Now that Annette was driving, her mom didn't hesitate to elicit her help such as this occasion to pick up some odds and ends. Annette was all too pleased to oblige. The world was, after all, rife with opportunities for an attractive young woman.

She walked up next to him as her mind was spinning through different ideas to start a conversation. He looked to be in his early twenties, tall, good-looking, and by himself.

She bumped him lightly with her hip, accidentally on purpose, as she was looking intently at items on the shelf. "Oh, I'm sorry."

"Oh, you're fine," he replied casually.

"Jeez, I'm trying to figure out which spaghetti sauce to get."

"I like this one," and he pointed to a jar on the shelf, "the tomato basil. I usually add it to some ground beef along with some seasonings."

"Sounds like you know how to cook."

"I've gotten more turned on to it since I started college and moved into an apartment. My name's Jack by the way."

"Oh, hi. I'm Annette." And she extended her hand.

Something about his expression told her that he was interested, but she wasn't sure what to say next.

"So, do you live in the area?" he inquired.

"Yes." But she wasn't about to reveal that she was a senior in high school living at home with her mom and dad. "What about you?"

"Yes, pretty close by actually. We should get together some time."

She tried to contain her excitement. "That would be great." And before she realized it, she also blurted out, "Let me have your phone number."

If it was an awkward moment for Annette, either he didn't notice or didn't seem to care because she had his number in the contact list of her cell phone when she left the store.

The next day when she had some time to herself out of earshot, she called his number. *That was easy*, she thought after plans had been made for a casual date later in the week. Now all she had to do was figure out what she was going to tell her mom and dad. That proved to be simple enough as well. She was getting together with some friends to eat on Wednesday evening. Except for the fact that it was Jack, whom she had just met, and not her friends, it was the truth. And they were fine with her plans as long as she was home by nine.

She was pretty well distracted for the rest of the week in anticipation of her date. She caught herself thinking about it from time to time and imagining what it would be like. But it was not something that she divulged to anyone else. The thought of getting to know him was not in her consciousness. Thoughts of making love to him were, and she found herself being aroused on more than one occasion. But she let it be and enjoyed the sensations. Taking herself there was something that never crossed her mind.

When she arrived that Wednesday just a few minutes after their appointed time, he was already there. She saw him waving from a booth in the corner and walked over.

"Hi, Jack. How are you?"

"I'm great. How about you?"

"Wow, this looks nice. I've not eaten here before."

"It's pretty casual, really. But the food is good."

She sat down next to him, giving him a brief touch on his shoulder with the palm of her hand as she eased herself into the seat. "So, what do you like here?"

"You," he replied. "Oh, that was really corny. I can't believe I just said that."

She laughed. "Not to worry, the feeling is mutual. So, what do like here on the menu?"

"There's a few things I like, but I think I'm gonna keep it kind of light tonight. The cobb salad is good, but it's actually a pretty good size."

"Oh, perfect. You want to share one of those?"

At that moment the waitress arrived and Jack spoke up, "We're going to share a cobb salad."

"Anything to drink?" she asked.

He ordered a draft beer and she had a glass of water with lemon. After showing his ID, the waitress was off to get their drinks. She sidled up closer to him and she felt him place his hand on her knee. *Yes.* And that touch elevated her already burbling sense of excitement.

"So, what do you like to do for fun?" she asked.

"You know," he said, "when I'm not involved in classes and all I've actually taken up intuitive massage."

"Really?" And she was captivated by the thought of being massaged.

"Yeah, there's a local school of integrative arts and they teach a number of classes related to massage therapy."

"Oh, that is so cool."

"It's really a very therapeutic way of relieving stress, muscular tension, and promoting relaxation."

"So, what does somebody wear when they get a massage?"

"It's typically done in the nude."

Her eyes widened.

He noticed her response and continued, "It's all very professional and strictly therapeutic. There's no, uh, how shall I say it? There's no intimate type of involvement. It's all very ethically oriented."

"Oh, of course," she responded as she placed her hand on his, which was still on her knee, and began lightly caressing with her fingertips. "So, what's the intuitive part?"

"That has to do with feeling, probing if you will, to find tension and anything else that might seem anomalous, out of place. You really have to know your anatomy and have a sense of what different areas of the body are supposed to feel like."

"Oh, jeez. It sounds much more involved than you might imagine it on the surface."

"It is."

"But, I mean if you were already involved with someone, you know, not a client . . . I mean it just sounds sexy to me."

And he gave Annette a coy smile as the waitress delivered their food and drink.

When they had finished their meal, Annette offered to pay, but he refused and gave the waitress a card.

"Thank you so much, Jack." She was full of anticipation, hoping that their evening was not over.

"You're so welcome," he said.

"Well it's still kind of early. I won't need to be home until nine."

"Would you like to come over for a little while?"

"Yes."

*

She was curiously relaxed as her eyes were closed and she lay naked face down across his bed. Her head was turned with her hands palm down on either side. She lay still and felt the coolness of the air on her bare bottom causing a sensation of excitement. The smell of coconut oil as Jack massaged her feet was an enticing element in this strange, wonderful event. She was becoming comfortable, but then she felt him rubbing coconut oil onto her calf. There was a constant pressure as he kneaded her calf with his forearm, slowly from the bottom upward, slowly up to just beneath her knee. Then he repeated it on the other calf. *Wow, that feels really good.* But this sensation of relaxation was transformed as she felt the soft warm wetness of his kiss lingering on her ankle. Now she felt his lips lightly caressing the back of her calf. He kissed her again farther up her calf. She had never been kissed there before, never been kissed like this. She was momentarily startled as she felt him place the palms of his hands on either side of her hips. The feel of his skin on her bare hips and the soft warmth of his kisses now on the back of her thigh were arousing her greatly. There was a pause, and she heard his movement behind her as she imagined that he was taking his clothes off. She felt him climb onto the bed and straddle her, and there was that wonderful kiss, now on the back of her neck. *Oh!* And she felt his hard dick brush the back of her leg. Another long, lingering touch of his lips right in the center of her back between her shoulder blades. She waited in suspense with her eyes closed, and there was the next one right in the hollow where her shoulder blade met the center or her back. *Yes.* He kissed her in the same spot on the other side. *Oh.* He was licking her there now. He kissed her again along her spine a little lower on her back. Another fleeting kiss a little farther down, and she waited, wondering what was next. There, she felt him pressing his lips into the small of her back as this aching tension grew stronger. Then there was a pause as he moved again, and her eyes opened as she felt the side of his face pressed against her bottom, pressed into the cheek of her ass where it met her leg as he firmly placed his hands back onto her hips. She closed her eyes again, and without thinking about it, she began pressing her groin into the bed. Her hips were moving ever so gently down into the firmness of the bed beneath her and then back up. And this feeling in her groin grew stronger as she began pressing herself harder into the bed. Her mind began to reel. *Oh God. Kiss me there, kiss me there.* Without her volition, her thoughts became words.

"Oh," she cried softly as she felt his lips lightly kissing her bottom.

Now he was kissing and slowly licking one side of her ass, then the other.

"Oh," she cried again as she felt his tongue caressing the crack of her ass.

There was no conscious thought as she spread her legs open. He moved his face down between her. His hands were now on the backs of her thighs, spreading her legs farther apart. *Oh my God.*

"Oh my God."

No one had ever kissed her there. And she started

coming as soon as she felt his tongue pressing between the lips of her pussy. Now she was arching her back and pressing her pussy into his face as his tongue found her clitoris and her orgasm crested over the top.

She relaxed her lower back and scooted herself away from him as she spoke in a bewildered state, "I came. I just came."

"Wonderful," he said in a soft voice.

She turned over on her side and saw his smile, but as soon as she spied his hard dick, she realized that she wasn't through. There it was, and she allowed herself to just stare at it for a moment. Then she rolled onto her back and just looked at his face, imploring him without a word. She spread her legs and he climbed between. He pressed just the tip of his dick between her wet lips.

"Oh," she cried again.

He just waited, and she was breathless in that moment, feeling the tip of his hard dick touching the entrance of her vagina. She waited, savoring the moment. He finally began pushing himself slowly into her and she placed her hands on his hips. She just lay still as she felt him going deeper and deeper, filling her up. Then they began to move. He slowly eased back out and she pulled her hips away from him. His dick was almost out when she reached down, pressing her hands onto the cheeks of his taut ass, driving herself back onto him. They kept moving, thrusting into each other, and with each thrust the aching in her groin became stronger. Now, she was clenching his dick as she began to move more rapidly, and she saw the look on his face. She clasped her pussy tightly around him as she moved her hips in short strokes. At the moment he cried out his release, she felt herself exploding into another orgasm even more intense than the first. Then she held perfectly still with his hard dick pressing against just the right spot inside her as this sexual sting held on and on and she was overcome with the sensation.

A few minutes later, Jack eased himself out of her, then propped himself up on one elbow beside her and whispered, "I'm sorry. That wasn't much of a massage, was it?"

Annette giggled.

SEVEN

For the next several days, Annette was ebullient. She wasn't in love. She didn't particularly care if she saw Jack again or not. But she was proud of her accomplishment. She was pleased that she could meet a really attractive young man, get him into bed, have great sex with him, and satiate her own burning desire. It gave her a sense of maturity, a sense of worldliness, like she was an experienced woman and not just a horny teenager.

She rode on this high without a care for a few weeks. And the moon went through its phases and came back around. Her cycle came back around too. It was feed-me fuck-me week and as usual she was most distracted by the fuck-me part.

She succeeded again at seducing a man. This one was a little older, but also very good-looking, very outgoing, and right up her alley. She couldn't believe that she'd seduced him and gotten involved all in the same day-all within an hour. She'd met him at a restaurant bar on the other side of town. She was supposedly going out to meet up with her friends on a Saturday night, to be home by eleven. But she never had any intention of meeting up with her friends. She was on the prowl. It was a bold move on her part. *But what the hell.* There was no reason a young woman couldn't enjoy the bar at a restaurant as long as she wasn't trying to get a drink underage. And she had no interest in drinking.

They landed at a nearby hotel only forty minutes after she'd first set foot in the bar and started chatting it up with some of the young men there. The two of them practically crashed through the door of the room as he hurled her onto the bed and started ripping his clothes off. He was so aggressive. This was nothing like her experience with Jack.

He lay on top of her on the bed, kissing her passionately. She was still fully clothed and he was totally naked. She could feel his dick getting hard, pressing against her leg as she held his head and kissed his mouth and his face. She was dying to take her clothes off too as she felt herself getting wet. He unbuttoned her blouse and started kissing her neck, and her chest. Caught up in the urgency of their heated encounter, she grabbed his hand and began caressing it with her mouth, licking between his fingers. Then she took one of his fingers and placed it in her mouth as she imagined she might place his hard dick there. She began sucking it, moving it in and out as she stroked his fingertip against her wet tongue. She felt him press his hard dick into her groin and her eyes fluttered open.

There it was. She was holding his left hand, the hand

she'd been making love to, and there it was. It was a band of light pigment around his ring finger. She froze.

She just lay there as he was grinding into her, and then she said, "Stop."

He was still for a moment and then asked quizzically, "What's the matter?"

"Are you married?"

He hesitated before he spoke. "Does it matter?"

She pushed him and he rolled onto his side. She stood up, buttoned her blouse, then looked down at him.

"Yes."

She turned and walked out.

*

Annette was fascinated with the whole process of seduction. Making love was a new wellspring of sensual discovery for her. Throughout the rest of her senior year in high school she looked for opportunities and discovered how easy it was for a beautiful, sexually charged young woman to get involved. Indeed, to culminate the process in relatively short order. Wining, dining, and getting to know one another were not necessary. She wanted to seduce attractive men and make love to them.

But there was one particular activity she had not yet experienced. She'd heard the term blowjob, and at some point came to the realization that it had nothing to do with actually blowing, and everything to do with oral stimulation. She had never kissed a man's penis, and it seemed to her like the most private, enticing, and exciting thing she could do. A man's penis was a secret part, yet when it became erect it became some type of banner, like a huge float in a parade, something that you just couldn't hide. She was becoming preoccupied with it and wanted to know it intimately.

There was another sexual encounter, another new experience, again unlike any of the others she'd had so far. She'd taken a trip by herself to the mall on the weekend to do some shopping when she saw him in the men's section of a department store. She was not shopping for men's clothes, she was shopping for a new date, and her creative mind had led her through that department. He was a large man in his late twenties, well over six feet tall, muscular with broad shoulders and a large chest.

"That's a beautiful suit," she exclaimed as she walked up to him.

"You think so?" he responded.

"Turn around."

He did as instructed.

"You've got to have the slacks hemmed, of course," she continued, "but it looks like it fits nicely. And I love the color on you."

She noticed that he wasn't wearing a wedding band and then took the opportunity to get her hands on him. Standing behind him, she reached up and pulled gently at the seams of the shoulders as if to straighten the material and then let one hand linger on his back.

"How does it feel?" she asked.

"The coat feels great. The waist of the slacks is great, but it's a little tight in the thighs."

She leaned closer, winked, and smiled. "Yeah, looks like you've been doing too many squats."

He smiled back at her.

"Let's try a larger waist size to accommodate the muscle in your thighs, and then you can have the waist taken in."

"Thank you so much. I really appreciate your help, ma'am."

"Oh, I don't work here. I just happened to be walking by, and you looked like a man in need."

He looked back at this vivacious young woman with a certain expression—a look that questioned what she meant by the double entendre.

"What size are those slacks?" she asked.

"They're a thirty-two."

She whispered, "Why don't you wait for me in the dressing room, and I'll see if I can find what you need."

He opened the door to the men's dressing room suite and walked in. She started scurrying around trying to find the right slacks in that size, but her mind was greatly distracted by the possibility of seducing him right then and there in the men's dressing room. She found the rack with the suit he was trying on and started riffling through the clothes. She found what she was looking for and walked over to the men's dressing room as she glanced from side to side. There was no one close by. She opened the door and quietly stepped inside, again looking around. She spied under the doors of the dressing room stalls. There was no one else there except him. She rapped lightly on his door, which was ajar.

"Yes," he responded.

She eased the door open to find him standing there naked with a wide-eyed look of anticipation. She handed him the slacks with one hand, reached down with her other hand, and grasped his soft penis. It immediately started to get stiff. His head fell back as he just stood there for a moment with his eyes closed, an ecstatic look on his face.

This was a moment she had been waiting for. She was not going to delay it, build up to it, or be coy about it. She was not going to miss this. She immediately peeled the leggings she was wearing down to her ankles and fell to her knees in front of him. She placed the palms of her hands on his legs, on either side of his groin, and just stared breathlessly at his penis inches from her face. It was turned downward, still not fully erect. She looked at his pubic hair, looked at his dick. She didn't want this moment to end.

He had tossed the slacks onto the seat behind him and was touching the back of her head lightly with his fingertips as she was lost in her adoration of this most private part of the man's anatomy. She finally reached over and clasped it with her left hand, her thumb pressing against the underside. She began squeezing it gently. She gasped a short breath as she closed her eyes and pressed her cheek against it. *Oh my God.* Now it was hard. She was so excited, she could feel her vagina becoming soaking wet. She opened her eyes and kissed it on the side, a long lingering kiss. She continued kissing it lightly down to the base of his shaft and nuzzled his pubic hair. Then she continued kissing her way back up toward the head of his dick. Without even thinking about it, her other hand had found its way to her own groin and was now lightly fondling her clitoris as she felt herself becoming more and more aroused. She froze for another moment on the verge of an orgasm with his hard dick in her face. She stopped stimulating herself momentarily as this feeling washed through her and subsided on the edge. Next she planted a kiss right on the tip of his dick, and then slowly pushed her mouth over it with her tongue pressed against the underside. She pressed the palm of her hand back onto her crotch, and this feeling in her groin started to grow again as she felt a man's dick in her mouth for the first time. She started a slow rhythm, moving the head of his dick in and out of her mouth as she began stimulating herself again. After a minute or so, she took his dick out of her mouth, moved to the underside, and began licking him right there where the foreskin meets the head. She was groaning out loud now as she began stimulating herself more vigorously. Then she began sucking him right there in the same spot. She heard him cry out as his dick started to spurt semen, and she wailed loudly as she began coming. Now she had a finger in her pussy as she was lost in the most intense orgasm she'd ever had.

A few moments later, she looked around, grabbed his underpants, and wiped the semen off of her shoulder. She was ebullient after this first experience of making love to a man's penis. She stood, pulled her leggings up, bounced up on her toes, and kissed him on the cheek. He was still standing there with a look of disbelief on his face when she smiled, turned, and walked out. When she opened the door of the dressing room suite, she was face-to-face with a short balding man standing there holding up a shirt on a hanger, a look of shock on his face having over-heard their flagrant expressions of sexual release. Annette giggled as she slid by.

EIGHT

Annette was having a good second semester during her sophomore year at college. She enjoyed her friends and her social life, too. But she had really taken to spending more of her free time in and out of some of the local bars in her quest for the next "date." That next one was really good-looking, with very curly, dirty blond hair, sparkling blue eyes, and a contagious smile. He seemed to have the usual qualities that she looked for when she picked up a guy. It was a lot of fun when it started, much flirtation and touching going on at the bar where they'd met. He'd had a bit to drink, but he didn't seem over the top. She never liked to kiss a guy in a bar, as much as she enjoyed kissing. It just seemed too tawdry. She never wanted to be that blatant in public. But there was a moment when she put her hand under the concealment of the table where they were sitting and placed it on his lap. She sat there smiling at him as the laughter and chatter of the people around them carried on. She began fondling him, and his dick started to get stiff beneath his jeans. Not too long after that they were on their way out of the door together, landing a few blocks away at his place.

When they walked in, the place was a wreck. Perhaps it was a typical college kid's digs with clothes strewn everywhere. But this place was really bad. There was dirt all over the floor in a hallway where someone had knocked over a potted plant and never bothered to clean it up. The poor plant looked like toast. She tried to ignore whatever the smell was coming from the kitchen. The cushions on the couch were askew, one of which was on the floor. She wondered whether the place had ever been vacuumed. And what was it with everything everywhere? Tools, books, magazines, ashtrays, dirty plates, empty beer bottles, popcorn on the floor. To call it an unkempt mess was too nice. It was tantamount to a trash pile.

She breathed a sigh of relief when they walked into his bedroom. It was relatively neat, and at least it wasn't filthy.

She dangled one arm around his waist, looked him in the eye, and said, "Nice place you've got here."

"Yeah, my roommates are pigs," he responded.

He pulled her in a little closer and began to kiss her. She was a little distracted by his beer breath. But he kissed her very gently so she put it out of her mind and began to enjoy his mouth. He reached behind her and put both hands on her ass. She pressed in closer and started moving rhythmically. She could feel his hard dick beneath his jeans pressing against her lower abdomen. She reached down and unbuttoned his jeans. In a few moments, she had his pants down to his knees and his dick in her hand. He unbuttoned her shirt and unhooked her bra, which had a clasp in the front.

He moved her shirt and bra on either side so he could look at her exposed breasts. "Your tits are so beautiful."

They weren't large, but they weren't too small. They sloped gently with a firm round shape beneath large dark brown nipples that were still soft. He just looked at her for a moment, then took his hands and started to pinch her nipples. It didn't feel good, it was actually a little painful the way he was tweaking them. She took the opportunity to move aside and remove her jeans. He immediately took his jeans off, got her onto the bed, and tried to get on top of her.

She resisted. "Wait a minute, you're going to need to put something on."

"Oh yeah," he replied.

She rolled him over on his side, got up, and fished a condom out of her purse.

"But, first," she said, and she laid the condom on the bedside table, looking down at his erect penis. She got back on the bed between his legs on her knees and began her usual worship. She closed her eyes and licked the underside of his dick. She cradled his balls with one hand while still licking his dick. She reached down with her free hand and began feeling herself when she felt something wet and sticky hit her eye as he groaned. *Oh my God! He's coming already!* She sat there for a moment contemplating what to do next, and she heard him begin to snore. *Oh my God! He's snoring!*

Sometimes the dates were okay. Sometimes the dates were really great. She'd had a mountaintop experience with a beautiful guy last month. His place was actually really nice. Neat. And clean. *He* was a nice lover—a really nice lover. She was thrilled with every moment of it. Even their departure after was pleasant. She also had her share of disappointments, if not disasters, like this latest one.

What was going on? Did she enjoy this? Was it fulfilling? There were no relationships. There was no intimacy. There was no caring or give or take beyond the sex. There was only her desire, her inexplicable compulsion, her fascination. She fed it, and it always came back for more. She was feeding her own black dog and didn't know it.

NINE

She was pissed. Leaving the nasty apartment of her would-be, now-snoring lover, she was pissed and determined. Determined to make it happen. She decided she needed a more upscale venue and went over to Ristorante Con Brio on the far side of campus. But it was late. There were very few people left in the place, and it looked like they were just about ready to close. She decided she might have to accept her fate and call it quits for the night. She sat down at the bar to order a stiff drink. That was something she didn't usually do because she was still underage. She did, however, have a fake ID that she used on occasion for emergency purposes, and there was no question at this point that she was having an emergency. She would have one drink to help her brood and then head home.

The bartender appeared from a back room behind the bar. He was a very good-looking young man with a twinkle in his eye, a smile on his face, a very flirtatious delivery, and no wedding band on his finger. She took one look at him and thought, *Okay, back to plan A.*

"And what would the beautiful young woman like to drink this evening?" he inquired.

When he returned with her drink, their fingers touched, and he smiled at her. There was no one else sitting at the bar, so he lavished his attention on her as he finished cleaning up.

"You know?" he said. "I was hoping to meet a beautiful woman tonight."

"Oh, stop."

"Really. I've actually met several tonight that expressed an interest, but I was holding out for you."

"Ha!" she snickered.

He kept on throwing out one-liners rife with sexual innuendo as she sipped her drink, and her peals of laughter rang throughout the bar. She was amused and attracted. He was attracted and almost done with work for the evening.

They landed at his place about thirty minutes later. It was very late, about two o'clock in the morning. His place was nice. What a relief. It was no luxury apartment, but it was clean and neat with soft lighting. He got himself a glass of white wine from a bottle in the refrigerator and asked if she'd like anything.

"Yes, but it's not in the fridge," she replied.

With that she put her arms around his waist, laced her fingers together, and they began to kiss. He had the glass of wine in one hand and his other hand on her shoulder. She reached down and placed her hand on his crotch. She could feel his dick underneath his jeans becoming stiff. He set the wine glass down on the counter and wrapped his arms around her, their kiss becoming more intense. They froze momentarily as their tongues touched lightly. He then reached down, unbuttoned, and unzipped her jeans. Then he slid both of his hands down her back beneath her underwear and placed one hand on each side of her ass. The feel of his hands gently rubbing her skin, and then his fingertips lightly pressing into the crease at the top of her thigh, turned up the aching in her groin. She rubbed his bulging jeans as he continued to caress her ass. She unbuttoned and unzipped his jeans. She reached in and took out his hard dick. In the meantime, his middle finger slid down the crack of her ass into her pussy, which was already wet. His finger found her wet lips and started a gentle circular motion. She reached down and moved his hand slightly onto her clitoris.

"Right there," she whispered.

He continued the motion with his finger as she explored his genitals with both hands. She was aching and on the verge of an orgasm. Just then he stopped and began removing the rest of his clothes and hers. He took a sip of his wine, took her by the hand, and led her into the living room. He got a condom out of a drawer on the table next to the couch and placed it on top of the table. She gave him a gentle push on his chest with her hands, and he lay back across the couch. She straddled his head, facing his belly. She just stayed there on her knees for a moment, her bare bottom directly above his head. He reached up and cupped her breasts with the palms of his hands. She spread her legs apart and eased down. He began kissing her pussy and licking her clitoris. He licked slowly up and down. She found his rhythm and moved her hips in time while looking down at his beautiful hard dick. She placed her hands on his hands as he continued massaging her breasts. She closed her eyes and started pressing herself into his mouth with more intensity. She finally leaned forward onto her elbows as he continued to lick her. She took one hand and placed his hard dick against her cheek and began to come again, finally finishing the orgasm that had started earlier. But she wasn't done. She began licking his dick and caressing it with her lips, with her tongue, with her mouth, and she was aching again. She then got up and put the condom on him. Now she straddled his hips, facing him. She eased herself down onto his hard dick and paused with only the head of his dick inside her. Then she leaned forward and they kissed and she started a very slow, easy rhythm. And little by little he went farther up inside her—a little farther, a little farther—until she had totally engulfed him. She clenched him and held his hard dick and started moving her hips up and down—up and down until he cried out his release. She clenched him and held him again. She moved her pelvis until she felt his still hard dick pressing against just the right spot inside her. She began moving ever so slowly as her tension rose higher and higher. She just kept that same motion, and the sensation became so strong that everything else began to disappear. He was moving in time to her rhythm.

"Don't stop," she moaned and it was coming, she could feel it coming, it was too late to stop now, and she started to shudder, having her next glorious orgasm. She finally collapsed with her head on his shoulder, lay there briefly, and thought, *That was a beautiful date*.

TEN

Annette sat in class fidgeting as the exams that had been graded were handed out. When her exam was placed on her desk face down, she flipped it over and looked in dismay at the score. *Sixty-seven? How did I get a sixty-seven?* she thought. It was the worst score she had gotten on any of her exams in any of her classes so far. She had been a very good, if not quite a straight A, student all along. But things had started to change this past semester. She made it to all of her classes and tended to most of her homework, but she was distracted. She wasn't getting *all* of her homework done, and she wasn't spending as much time studying and preparing for exams.

When class was over, she went to the snack bar for lunch, still ruminating about her low test score. She bought something to eat and sat down, her mind lost in thought. She had started studying for the exam last week but hadn't made it through all of the material and hadn't devoted as much time as she usually did. She had planned on studying the night before the exam, too, but didn't do a very good job of it.

The day before the exam on her way home from her

last class, she ran into a guy she knew, a very good-look-ing guy. It was a lover from one of her "dates." He had been one of the really good ones. He recognized her, and they stopped to chat. She had every intention of getting something to eat and then hitting the books, but she found herself flirting with this guy instead. The more she flirted, the more she thought about the last time they'd been together. The more she flirted, the more they touched, and the more aroused she started to become. She knew she had to study for the exam, but this flirta-tion, this arousal, this desire was taking over, and now she was trying to seduce him. She told herself she'd have time to study after she was done with him.

About twenty minutes after they'd crossed paths, they were at his place. She teased him mercilessly. After she got his pants halfway down and played with his dick long enough to get it good and hard, she pushed him back onto his bed. Then she started to undress. First, she took off her blouse and her bra just so she could watch his face as he stared at her tits. She straddled him on the bed and leaned her torso forward and dangled her tits in his face, never allowing them to touch his face, and not allowing him to touch them. This was just one of the many games she liked to play. Next, she stood back up on the floor, faced away from him, and slowly took her jeans down so he could see her ass. She stood there with her jeans and her underwear halfway down her legs and looked over her shoulder as he admired her bare bottom. She placed one hand on either side of her ass with her middle fingers in the crease at the top of her legs on either side. She pulled her ass cheeks apart for him to see. She was still watching his face, enthralled with his response. Then she straddled him again, this time facing his belly with her ass above his face. She swatted his hands away and giggled when he reached up and tried to touch her.

"Not yet," she said.

She put her hands on her ass again and very slowly and deliberately separated her ass so he could see everything she had. She looked over her shoulder again down at his face to see that he was totally enraptured. Then she turned her head forward and looked down to admire his beautiful hard dick. She slowly eased herself down, putting her bottom closer and closer to his face. She finally leaned forward, closed her eyes, took one hand, and pressed his hard dick against her cheek. Then she began her lovemaking in earnest.

She pressed her pussy onto his mouth and said, "Now."

She continued kissing and licking his dick, but was very careful not to arouse him too much. She wanted to turn him on as much as she could without allowing him to come. She came while caressing his dick with her mouth. She came again later when they fucked. She had a third and final glorious orgasm stimulating herself while caressing his soft penis with her mouth after he had come.

It was a lovemaking session that lasted at least an hour and a half and left them both beautifully satiated. They had both fallen asleep. She awoke several hours later with her face pressed against his soft penis. She bolted up, got dressed, gathered her books, and ran home.

The entire way home she was muttering to herself, "Damn it, Annie! Damn it, Damn it, DAMN IT! Why did you do that?"

When she got home, she put on some coffee and attempted to study. It was not one of her best efforts.

She sat there at the snack bar after reflecting on the night before the exam. She knew that not only had she allowed herself to get distracted by her seduction, ruining her efforts to prepare for the exam, but that it was the third time this week she had seduced and made love to someone.

ELEVEN

Annette was overdue for a trip home and a brief respite from schoolwork as well as her usual college life. She had come home Friday night after her last class to see her mom and dad. But a visit with her old friend Mrs. Baker was also definitely in order. She just couldn't come home and not see her while she was there. Firstly, if Annette did come home, not visit with Mrs. Baker, and she found out about it, she would be pissed. That would not stand. But more importantly, Annette dearly loved the old woman and wouldn't miss the opportunity to spend a little time with her whenever she was in town. Flossie Baker was in the kitchen that Saturday morning when Annette rang the doorbell.

Annette heard the old woman's voice from behind the front door. "Coming . . ." As soon as she opened the door, she exclaimed, "Oh, my, my, it's been too long! Come in."

Annette smiled. "Hello, Mrs. Baker." And they immediately fell into a heartfelt embrace.

"Oh, it's so good to see you. Don't you look lovely. Please come sit in the kitchen, and I'll fix us some coffee."

"That would be great."

Annette followed her through the hallway and paused at the long, narrow console table, which was overflowing with family photos. She saw a portrait that she'd never noticed before in all the years she'd been in and out of Mrs. Baker's home.

"Oh, wow! Who's this, Mrs. Baker? Is that Claire? She's beautiful."

"Oh, honey. That's me when I was nineteen."

Annette looked at her and laughed with surprised glee as they continued into the kitchen. They sat down at the nook table in front of a row of windows as the morning sun came beaming in.

Mrs. Baker was an older woman when Annette first met her as a young child, but now she seemed to be showing her age. Her gait was slower, her posture not as erect, and her hair mostly gray. Annette thought it was remarkable that she still lived alone in that big house, but she had a good network of people that she stayed in touch with: Annette's mom and dad, other people in the neighborhood, and quite a few people from the church that Mrs. Baker had been a part of for so many years. She was well connected socially.

They sat enjoying their coffee and each other's company.

"So, how is college life?" Mrs. Baker asked.

"Oh, I'm doing really well. I had a three point seven grade point average last semester."

Annette went on to explain what a grade point average

was.

Mrs. Baker looked at Annette with that twinkle in her eye and said, "How's college *life*?"

Annette, a little startled, was immediately concerned that perhaps there was some decline in her mental faculty.

Flossie immediately responded, "Oh, honey, please. Don't look at me like I've got dementia or something. It's great that you're getting good grades and all, but what's college *life* like? I mean, have you met anybody?"

Annette just giggled, realizing that dear old Flossie hadn't lost a thing as far as her mental character was concerned.

Mrs. Baker continued, "Oh, honey, you're so lovely. I'm sure the young men are lined up around the block."

Annette was at a loss to respond. "Well," she finally said, "I haven't really met anybody just yet."

"Well, maybe you should let that grade point average slide a little bit and concentrate on the important things."

Annette giggled again, but Flossie wasn't giving up that easily.

"Well, I know there must be someone that you've spent time with. It doesn't always work out and sometimes that's a good thing."

And there was an unusual silence between them as the sage old woman just waited for the next response.

Annette, in a moment of truth, revealed just enough. "I've dated a number of guys, Mrs. Baker, but nobody I really wanted to keep seeing."

"Uh huh," was her only response as she stroked her chin and looked into Annette's face.

After a few moments, they changed the subject and finished their coffee. As their visit drew to a close, Flossie walked with Annette to the front door. They hugged.

Then Mrs. Baker held Annette at arm's length as she looked her in the eye and said softly, "We have our needs, dear. Just be careful. There's more important things."

Annette glanced down and nodded her head. Then she looked back up and smiled, "G'bye, Mrs. Baker."

TWELVE

Annette was back at Ristorante Con Brio on the other side of campus having a light dinner with a couple of her classmates. She made it a point to eat light if she was going to be in pursuit. That thought had crossed her mind before she left her apartment. Never mind that she was going out with her girlfriends; she still had her agenda. She was casually noticing possibilities even as she sat chit chatting and laughing with her friends. They didn't usually eat at this restaurant because it was a little pricy, but they had taken their old chum, Cindy, out to celebrate her birthday on a Friday night. Cindy's birthday was actually on Saturday, but she was going to be at home with her family for the rest of the weekend.

They sat in the middle of the large ornate room with a marble floor and huge marble columns around the perimeter. The room had a great high ceiling, which had a huge dome of stained glass in the center. There were lush live-potted plants at various locations around the room in large colorful pots. The tables had burgundy tablecloths and the whole place reeked of opulence and elegance. It was very crowded on a Friday night and everywhere was the movement of waiters, busboys, and diners moving about between the tables.

She spied the object of her affection *du soir* about midway through the meal but made no mention of it to the others. The man Annette had seen was a bit older, perhaps in his late twenties. He'd finished a meal by himself and was having another drink. She hadn't looked directly at him, but she'd seen him notice her a couple of times out of the corner of her eye. He was attractive and seemed to have a very pleasant and confident demeanor when talking with his waitress. Annette was dressed in a short skirt that revealed enough of her long legs, which she casually displayed for the gentleman she was interested in. She intentionally dressed to look good, if not provocative, when she was going out on her quest for a date, and this evening was intended to be more than a birthday celebration for Cindy.

When Annette and her friends broke up to go their separate ways, she said goodbye to everyone and gave Cindy a big hug. "See you later, Cindy, and happy birthday, girlfriend."

It was a warm heartfelt embrace between two very close long-time buddies. Cindy had always confided her biggest secrets to Annette, and Annette had always been a good listener and a close friend. Yet there was a distance; Annette kept her own secrets to herself and had not shared the same details of her life that Cindy had shared with her.

As everyone was walking out, Annette ducked into the women's room.

When she came out, he was looking directly at her, and as if on cue he said, "Would you care to join me?"

She smiled and sat down next to him at his table. At this point in her social trajectory, she much preferred guys who knew how to get down to business. She could never be absolutely sure at first, but this looked like a man who knew what he wanted. There was the usual conversation about how nice the food was and all that. But there he was with his face a little too close to hers, in her space. Yet he seemed relaxed, like he would be perfectly content if she were to get up and leave. She looked for that in a spontaneous date. She looked for someone who was interested, who gave clear signals, but who could take it or leave it and move on with no problem. So far, he was scoring very highly, and she had become fairly aroused by more than one flirtatious touch they'd shared so far. Even so, she didn't give too much of her excitement away, not just yet. He indicated that he was in town for some type of business trip and was staying at the Windsor Inn, which was very close to one of her favorite hangouts, The Applegate. She had declined his offer for a drink because she was still underage, but within about a half an hour, the deal was sealed and they were on their way to his room for a drink there.

She took a casual look around as they stepped into his room at the Windsor Inn. It wasn't exactly upscale. It was clean, it was fine, but maybe not as nice as she might have expected. But the game was on regardless of the accommodations. He asked if she liked Scotch, and she said yes. She'd had her first drink when she was in high school. Mostly the usual shenanigans with schoolmates. She had abused it a couple of times and regretted it the next day, but typically didn't overdo it anymore. At this point, she enjoyed drinking socially, but it wasn't her thing. Her thing was right there in the dress slacks of the man she was with.

She draped one arm around his waist and planted a kiss on his cheek as he poured their drinks. She took a glass from his hand and took a long drink as he stepped closer. It was the first drink she'd had in a while. It felt warm going down, and before long, she started to feel a bit tipsy. She lifted her skirt and pressed herself close to him. She could feel his dick becoming hard through his slacks on her bare hip. They began to kiss, all very nice at first.

They began to undress each other, and after she unzipped his pants, she stepped back and said, "Why don't you show me what you've got?"

She stood there with her hands on her hips and watched as he took his pants down. When she saw his pubic hair, she felt that feeling and began to get wet. And there it was, nice and hard just the way she liked it. It certainly wasn't the biggest one she'd seen, but he was well appointed, and it was beautiful. She gave him a playful little push on his bare chest with her hands, and he sat back on the bed directly behind him. She grabbed a pillow from the bed and threw it on the floor between his legs. She got down on her knees, taking her time savoring the moment, moving in closer to his hard dick. She closed her eyes just as she planted that first kiss on the tip of his dick. She felt his large, strong hands on her shoulders as she began licking him.

He groaned and began to speak in a low voice. "Oh, you like that, don't you? You're such a beautiful slut."

Her eyes flew open and she froze. She'd never been called a slut before and immediately knew that she didn't like it. He rubbed her shoulders and after a brief pause, she took the head of his dick into her mouth.

He moved one of his hands behind her head and began to speak again. "Oh, you love that, don't you, baby? All you sluts love that cock."

She was totally distracted now and really didn't think she wanted to continue, but his hand kept her head in place, and she really couldn't move too much. She thought about trying to bite him but didn't want to hurt him. So she waited for a moment and finally wriggled free.

She stood up and said, "You know, I'm sorry, but I think we're done."

In a moment, he was on his feet, and he slapped her across the face, hard. Before she could react, he grabbed her by the shoulders, spun her around, and threw her on the bed.

She was completely taken by surprise and cried out, "What are you doing?"

"I'm giving you what you deserve, slut. Don't say another word."

She began to get up, and he hit her on the cheek with his fist so hard that it spun her head to the side and she was thrown down on her back by the blow. For a moment, she thought that she might black out. Now he was on top of her with one hand over her mouth.

"Just relax, and I'll give you what you came for."

She just lay there completely terrified.

"Don't say another word or I'll beat the shit out of you, slut." He then moved his crotch in closer to her face and pressed his hard dick against the cheek that he'd hit, that was bleeding, that was still stinging with pain.

"And don't try to bite me either or you will *not* wake up tomorrow."

Then he grabbed her face with one hand and put the tip of his hard dick against her lips.

"Suck that dick, slut."

And she took him into her mouth as tears rolled down her cheeks. After what seemed like an eternity, he started to groan and then came in her mouth, forcing himself into her even harder. She couldn't breathe and started to gag as the hot semen spurted down her throat, but she couldn't move. Tears were streaming down her face. When he sat back on her chest with all his weight, he was so heavy that she could barely breathe.

She opened her eyes, which had been squeezed shut, and he said, "Did you like that?"

She didn't answer.

He slapped her across the face and shouted, "Did you like that?"

She nodded her head tentatively with tears streaming out of her eyes as he brought his hand back as if he were going to slap her again. She flinched, squeezing her eyes shut. He finally got up, got dressed in silence, and left her there on the bed. She was too stunned, too traumatized to even think about calling the police. She just lay there sobbing.

She finally got up, put her clothes on, clutched her purse, stumbled out of the room, and found her way back out onto the street. She had no clue what she was going to do or where she was going when she saw a very large black man approaching her.

THIRTEEN

Tom saw that the woman was unsteady on her feet and, after getting a few steps closer, immediately recognized her. He ran up to her and delicately put his huge arms around her so that she wouldn't fall.

"Oh, baby, what's happened to you?" he said in his low, calm voice.

But before she could respond, he'd already made the call and could hear a faint voice coming from his cell phone, "Nine-one-one, what's your emergency?"

"I need an ambulance at the corner of Applegate and Pine," he responded.

"Don't call the police," Annette said.

She didn't know why, she was just too shocked and embarrassed to cope. She wished he hadn't called an ambulance, either, but it was too late for that.

He finished the call with the 911 operator and put his phone away.

"Who did this to you?" he asked.

She replied in a tearful voice, "I don't know."

"Where is he?" he shot back.

"I don't know. He's long gone."

And she began to cry. He shook his head ever so slightly and put his arms back around her to comfort her and keep her upright. There was no place comfortable to sit down.

They stood there for what seemed the longest time. It was late, and Tom had been on his way home from The Applegate. She felt the warmth of his body as he held her in a gentle embrace, but she couldn't stop shivering. She didn't know what had happened. She'd had some unpleasant experiences with men before, and even walked out on a couple of dates that had seemed very promising at the start. But she'd never in her young life experienced the wrath and fury of a man who hated provocative women. Finally, she heard the sound of an ambulance in the distance.

When they wheeled her into the emergency room, she was still in a daze. Unfortunately for her, it was a busy night in the emergency room and her condition, however terrible it seemed to her, was not life threatening. She gave her ID and insurance card to Tom, who took care of her admittance. He returned with a clipboard, and she signed several forms. When Tom returned again, he dropped the cards into her purse and zipped it closed. He sat down across from her. And so they waited. He sat expressionless, his huge torso leaned forward with his elbows on the arms of the chair and his hands in front of him with one hand wrapped around the fist of the other. They did not speak. He did not ask. He looked at her softly in quiet, and they waited.

There was a pretty steady stream of people coming in during that night as they continued to wait. About an hour after they got there, a tall thin young man walked through the sliding doors into the emergency room. He got about halfway to the reception desk, stopped dead in his tracks, and then spewed vomit all over the place. Tom glanced over with a look of disgust on his face, and then the young man fell straight forward onto the concrete floor. Annette couldn't believe what she was seeing or hearing. The sound of his head hitting the floor made her wince. A moment later, two of the medical staff rushed over.

One of them was an older woman with a weary face, and she said to no one in particular, "These things always happen on a full moon."

Finally, a nurse came to get Annette and helped her back to an examination room. She took her pulse, checked her blood pressure, and asked several questions while taking notes.

"The doctor will be in shortly," she said and left the room.

Again Annette waited. Finally, the doctor came in and examined her, asking more questions. He cleaned up her cheek, which was now severely bruised. He then put some kind of gel and a bandage on.

"You should be fine. You can put an ice pack on there to reduce the swelling, and you can take the bandage off tomorrow. Take some aspirin if you need to for any pain. I'll get someone to help you out of here."

The doctor left and somebody else in hospital garb arrived a few minutes later. The woman helped her into a wheelchair. Tom stood up as she was being wheeled out, got out his cell phone, and contacted an Uber. The woman waited with them and helped her into the car when it arrived.

She made sure Annette had her seat belt on and then said softly to Annette, "You need to be more careful about the company you keep."

Annette's social trajectory had been suddenly, radically, and irrevocably taken off course.

FOURTEEN

When they arrived back at Annette's apartment near the edge of campus, Tom helped her out of the car and escorted her inside. He sat down in her living room, his huge frame making the chair look like a child's toy.

"Have you got something to write with?" he asked.

She walked into the kitchen area, got a small pad and a pen, and gave it to Tom. She sat down with her legs curled up on the couch across from him, looking bewildered.

"What did he look like?" Tom asked.

"I don't know. I don't want to talk," she said.

Tom knew of another young woman. He had not witnessed the aftermath of that event, but she had suffered a similar fate at that same hotel. He suspected that it had been the same man.

"This ain't all about *you*," he said. "This has happened before. We got a situation that needs to be rectified. What did he look like?" he repeated, his left hand crooked awkwardly around the pen, which appeared tiny, dangling over the pad he held in the other hand.

"I don't remember."

He looked at her incredulously with eyebrows raised and cocked his had to one side. Slowly and deliberately he said, "Was he short or tall?"

"About medium."

"Maybe five tenish?"

"Yes."

"Was he fat? Skinny?"

"He wasn't fat, kind of stocky."

Tom's left hand was scribbling on the pad. "What about his hair?"

"Yes, he had hair."

He gave her that same look. "Was it long, short, curly, straight?"

"It was straight, kind of short."

"Thin, balding?"

"No, thick, kind of a light brown."

"This was a white dude?"

"Yes."

"Any other ethnicity that you noticed?"

"No, just a white dude."

And so the question and answer continued.

Finally, Tom asked, "Anything else about this guy? Anything unusual, tattoos? Anything stand out?"

"No. Yes. He had really big hands."

She sat there and just looked at him quizzically for a moment. "Where are you coming from with all of this? I mean, you sound like a detective or something."

He looked up from the notepad and said, "When I'm not

bouncing or doing martial arts, I'm studying. Criminology. At the community college."

As she sat there in the aftermath of the crisis, Annette experienced an epiphany. For perhaps the first time in her life, she started to have an appreciation for the depth of people, random people that you meet, that maybe you don't think twice about.

He stood up to leave and got out his cell phone. She suddenly felt so alone.

"Don't leave," she said.

"I got to go, Annette. Savannah gonna whup my ass."

"Who's Savannah?"

"My woman."

"I didn't know you were married."

"Not, but just as well be."

And before she knew it, he had gone. She got up from the couch, found her purse, and pulled out her cell phone. She stopped with tears in her eyes. She wanted to call Cindy. Tell her everything—everything that had happened, everything she had never told her before. But she wasn't going to ruin Cindy's birthday weekend.

She just stood there exhausted, confused, her eyes soaking wet, her mind screaming, *Slut! Fucking slut! Why are you such a fucking slut?*

FIFTEEN

He was a tall, thin, attractive young man in his early twenties with green eyes and sandy blond hair that curled up around the back of his neck. She was a beautiful woman with piercing blue eyes and red hair. They walked into her bedroom, and she motioned for him to sit down on a chair. Then she stood facing him and began to undress. It was a performance that she had done many, many times before. All part of the prelude. She unbuttoned her blouse slowly and took it off. Her thick, long red hair cascaded around her bare shoulders. She reached behind her back and unhooked her bra, dropped it to the floor, and stood there bare breasted, allowing him a brief view. Then she turned around, looking over her shoulder at him. Her jeans were skin-tight, and the young man sat there transfixed at the view. She slowly unbuttoned and unzipped her jeans. She moved her hips from side to side and slowly pushed her jeans and panties down. She got about halfway down her hips with the crack of her ass showing and paused. She pushed her jeans down a little farther so that he could now see the bottom of her ass, the crease on either side where her legs met her cheeks.

She waited for a moment, letting him take it in, then she turned around, removed her jeans, and sat naked on the edge of the bed. She leaned back onto her elbows and slowly parted her legs.

He looked at her from a short distance across the room where he was still sitting. She was surprised to catch his gaze knowing what all men wanted to see at a time like this. Most men never looked into her eyes at all.

He was thrilled watching her undress, and he had looked at her pussy, too, as she sat there on the edge of the bed, gazing at it several times. She was unshaven with thick red pubic hair in tight curls that made a perfect triangle. His eyes moved slowly up her legs to her inner thighs, then to her lower abdomen, to her pubic hair, and then into the parted lips of her vagina. He was extremely aroused. He had never seen a real woman's pussy before. But his gaze kept returning to her eyes. He stood up, walked over, then knelt down in front of her. But when he leaned in to kiss her, she turned her head away.

He felt confused, but when she said, "Well, do you want it or not?" he was completely deflated.

Something about the sarcasm in her tone of voice. He didn't know what to do at this point. He was too naïve to realize that he'd been set up by his friends with a prostitute. There was nothing between the two of them; they'd only just met earlier that evening. But he was thrilled when she came on to him. He was so taken, yet so awkward around beautiful women. He had a hard time talking to them, and had a difficult time getting involved, never mind getting laid. So here was another failed sexual encounter for this young man who wanted nothing more than to be sexually involved with a beautiful woman. Jeremy felt like he would be an eternal virgin.

*

Jeremy was an only child who grew up with his mom in a single-parent home. His mother and father had divorced when he was young. His father took off, never made contact, and never paid any child support. He and his mom lived in a two-bedroom apartment. She did secretarial work and did her best to make a decent income, provide a home, and take care of her son. It was no small feat for a woman on her own of limited means, but she made do. Jeremy always had a comfortable home and food on the table.

Jeremy was kind of reclusive as a youngster. Sure, he went to school and had friends. But he spent most of his free time in the privacy of his room, playing the guitar. He had an older friend at school named Bill who had been playing the guitar for a few years. They would get together from time to time, and he would show Jeremy different things, including how to play various chords, eventually teaching Jeremy the basics of scales. They would typically get together on weekends. It was like he was getting private lessons, at least on an intermittent basis, which was great for Jeremy since his mother couldn't afford to spend the money on a private teacher. Bill was taking private guitar lessons, and he seemed to love nothing more than to pass what he had learned along to Jeremy. Jeremy would go home after meeting with Bill and try out all of the things his friend had taught him. Jeremy would also sit for the longest time listening to his favorite songs and trying to duplicate what he heard on the guitar. Over a period of years, he actually got good at it and developed a very strong foundation as a guitarist.

He also turned into an accomplished singer who not only had a strong voice, but knew how to find a harmony part. He sang in the choir at school and enjoyed that as well as learning to sing his favorite songs while accompanying himself on guitar. He played acoustic guitar, he played electric guitar, and he had started writing songs in his teens.

There were some other kids he knew at school during his early teens that shared his interest in music. One of them, Jay, played the drums and lived in a neighborhood close by. He kept his drums set up in the basement, which had enough space for rehearsals. Jeremy and some of his friends from school started hanging out on weekends at Jay's, learning songs and playing music together. Their first gig together as a band was at the school talent show. It was before Jeremy had joined the school choir, and it was his very first time performing in front of an audience—an experience Jeremy would never forget.

There's something about that first time someone performs in front of an audience. It's something no musician ever forgets.

There was a dress rehearsal in the afternoon the day of the show. They got there early and moved all the equipment in, getting set up as best they could off to the side. Then they waited while all of the other acts moved on and off the stage and ran through their performances. There were quite a few singers, all of them singing along with prerecorded music. There were a variety of other acts, too, but theirs was the only live band. It was all so exciting. Their turn came during the rehearsal and they moved everything out onto the stage, got tuned up, and then waited for their cue. The curtain opened, the lights went on, and they launched into their first song. They played a total of three songs, about ten or fifteen minutes worth of music. They pulled that much off, and everyone in the band was enthused about the performance coming up that night. Theirs was the last performance of the rehearsal.

The director of the talent show announced as they were getting ready to leave, "Okay, everybody, great work today. The show is at seven-thirty tonight. Be back here behind stage by seven. Not seven-thirty! Not seven-fifteen! Seven o'clock, people!"

Later that evening, when Jeremy arrived back at school with his mom before the performance, there was a commotion of people moving about, talking and laughing as everyone was filing into the auditorium and getting a seat. The place was very crowded, if not packed. Jeremy couldn't believe all of the people. His mom wished him good luck, and he went backstage to the designated spot where their equipment was set up and ready to go. He was there with his other friends in the band, but he was not himself. He couldn't believe how nervous he was. Little did he realize that everybody else was going through pretty much the same experience. His stomach was in knots, and his hands were shaking.

Jay looked over at him and laughingly said, "Man, you look scared *shitless*."

One of the teachers helping out with the show happened to walk up, and Jay's face immediately fell, assuming he was going to get detention or something for cursing, but the teacher had more important things on her agenda.

She patted Jeremy on the back, smiled, and said, "Take a few deep breaths." She paused and spoke again calmly. "Just breathe. You guys sounded great today at the rehearsal."

She glanced over and looked at Jay over the top of her glasses with a knowing look, smiled, and walked away.

Their time came and as soon as the previous performer left the stage and the curtain closed, they moved their equipment out into place. Jeremy rolled out his amp, went back, took the guitar off the stand, and put his head through the strap, adjusting his collar underneath the strap. He had double-checked the tuning of his guitar just a few minutes before. He took a deep breath and walked out on stage. He found the guitar cord that was already plugged into the amp and plugged it into his guitar. Finally, he turned the amp on and double-checked all the settings on the guitar and the amp. He looked up, and everyone else was pretty much in place. Jay made a few final adjustments on his drum set, and they were ready. Jeremy nodded at the stagehand working the curtain. When the curtain went up and the stage lights came on, Jay counted off the first song, and they started to play. Jeremy played the guitar and closed his eyes as he sang. He could hear the sound of his own voice coming back through the monitor speaker. He found himself lost in the moment, singing his heart out, totally enthralled with making those sounds with his own voice. He opened his eyes under the glare of the lights up there in front of all the people and felt an exhilaration he'd never known. He was on a journey. His performance was his own private journey, and he took them all with him. When they finished the first song, the auditorium exploded into applause.

That was the birth, the start of his love affair with performing. There seemed to be no end of the comments he got from different students and teachers the following week at school.

"Hey, Jeremy! You a rock star, dude!" was his greeting when he arrived at school the following Monday morning from a guy he'd seen around but had never actually spoken to before.

Moments later, as he was walking through the hall, two younger girls watched him approaching, then turned away to face each other, giggling when he saw them.

Later that same day, a friend of his he shared several classes with made a point to speak, "I never even knew you played guitar or sang. How long has that been going on?"

"Great performance at the talent show, Jeremy. I mean, great performance!" was the next comment he received when crossing paths with the same teacher that had been there just before the show.

He was dumbfounded by the end of the day. He'd never had so much attention around school. But more significant than his glimmer of fame was the transformation that would proceed. What started out as the most nerve-racking experience of his life would morph into one of the greatest joys. The anxiety of being up there in front of a crowd turned into the anticipation and excitement of live performance, something he would get better and better at.

SIXTEEN

Jeremy's mom never talked about Jeremy's father, never said anything negative about him, and never explained what had happened to their marriage. Jeremy couldn't have known directly, but she was bitter about her divorce, and perhaps had her own confusion and lack of rapport with men in general. At one point, she had taken on a new position as a secretary and one of the older men in the office had come on to her. Jeremy's mother was certainly attractive enough to get the attention of men at that point in her life, but the whole interaction didn't sit well with her. All Jeremy remembered as a young teenager was how she spoke of the experience when she came home that evening from work. She was terribly caustic about it and couldn't believe that the man was flirting with her and had touched her. He had touched her on the waist right there in the office. Her reactions such as this one had an impact, and Jeremy would avoid trying to flirt or engage in any type of sexual interaction with girls that he was attracted to.

High school had been kind of tough for him even though he generally got pretty good grades and was active with his music. He was a nice guy that got along easily with almost everybody, but he was usually too shy to speak to the girls that interested him most. His only sexual outlet was his own fantasy and his own stimulation. He was incredibly curious and interested in the opposite sex, but he didn't have the social skills, the confidence, or the bravado that worked for other guys.

There was one girl in high school that he took out shortly after he'd gotten his driver's license. She was a cute short-haired blonde who shared a couple of his classes. One day in class, they started talking about a song they'd heard on the radio and shared a connection with that. He asked what she was doing Saturday night, and she mentioned a movie that she wanted to see, so they made plans to go to the movies. When he picked her up, she was wearing a short skirt, nothing too revealing, but when she crossed her legs, he could see the curve of her thigh and was very turned on. The movie was fun, but not as memorable as her legs. When he drove her home, she invited him in. She said that her dad was home, but that he was upstairs sleeping. So they got cozy on the carpet with a couple of pillows in the living room, which was very close to the staircase leading upstairs. In short order, she had taken off her sweater and revealed her breasts. She sat there next to him. Her breasts were so beautiful. She had light soft skin and soft pink nipples. He leaned forward and pressed his cheek against one of her breasts. Just the feel of her soft skin was intoxicating, and as he breathed in, he could smell the scent of her skin. He began to kiss her breast on the underside right there in the crease where the roundness of her breast met her torso. At that moment, he thought he heard a sound coming from upstairs. He was so nervous about her father coming down the stairs and catching them that he couldn't continue. So before long he said goodnight and left. It was all pretty awkward, and she never really connected with him after that. It seems he'd always thought in terms of getting involved with someone and the concept of a one-night stand was foreign to him. He berated himself for missing out. He remembered how beautiful her tits were and regretted that he didn't have the guts to finish what had been started. He regretted that he didn't get laid. But the truth was probably more that she was just carefree and not looking for a relationship or a one-night stand. She was just an inexperienced high school girl who had shown her tits to Jeremy, but he couldn't just enjoy it for what it was and let it go from there.

*

By the time Jeremy entered the music department at college, he not only had a solid musical foundation as a guitarist and as a singer, but he'd had quite a bit of experience performing. College life kept him busy. There wasn't too much free time. He was either in class, doing homework, studying, practicing guitar, or involved in music otherwise. This included playing out pretty regularly with a band that he'd gotten into after starting college. They played at several different venues, including a couple of local bars like The Applegate, which was close by.

As much as he loved performing, he almost never worked up the courage to speak to any of the girls that were in attendance. And when he did, they either blew him off, were with somebody else, or were gone by the time the gig was over.

There was one occasion on a break between sets that an attractive girl spoke to him as he was getting a glass of ice water at the bar.

"I'm loving the way you guys sound," she said.

"Oh, thanks."

"My name's Julie," and she extended her hand.

Jeremy shook her hand with a blank look on his face and stammered, "Hi, I'm Jeremy."

She asked how long he'd been playing guitar, and he began to talk about his history with the guitar. He asked if she also played music, to which she replied no, but then spoke of her classes and involvement there at the college. It was a simple enough dialogue, but it was a struggle for him to remain calm and collected in her presence.

"I've got to go," he said.

Just as he turned to walk back up to the bandstand, she touched him on the shoulder and said, "Wait."

She reached into her purse, fished out a scrap of paper and a pen, scribbled her number on it, and handed it to him with a smile. He took the piece of paper, folded it, and placed it in his shirt pocket.

The next day, he picked up his cell phone and set it on the desk. He retrieved the phone number of the girl he'd met the night before and then sat there, too tortured by his own insecurity with women to make the call. *What if she doesn't remember me?* he thought. *What if I ask her out and she says no?* And so his unruly mind went on and on with all the unnecessary questions and all of the doubt, too afraid of the failure and too caught up in the anxiety to realize that even if he failed somehow, even if it didn't work out, even if he embarrassed himself and fell flat on his face, it would never matter! So what? So what if he fell flat on his face? But that thought never crossed his mind. He never made the phone call.

SEVENTEEN

Cindy enjoyed her birthday weekend at home. It was great to see her mom and dad and her brother Paul. They mostly hung around the house and enjoyed some great meals, not to mention birthday cake and all the rest. She was sorry that her boyfriend, Brad, couldn't be part of it, but she'd catch up to him when she returned to school Sunday night.

On the way back that Sunday night she answered her cell phone while driving but didn't recognize the voice at first.

"I'm sorry, who's this?" she asked and Annette said, "Cindy, it's Annette!"

Cindy answered back with a worried tone in her voice. "Sweetie, what is the matter? Are you okay?"

"No, I'm not."

"Well, I was on my way to Brad's place."

"Please, come over," Annette implored.

"Okay, let me call Brad and let him know I won't see him till later. I'll be there soon."

When Cindy arrived and knocked on the door, it opened almost straight away. Annette just stood there, but Cindy took one look at her face and wrapped her arms around her.

"What happened to your cheek?" Cindy asked.

"It's a long story." Annette wasn't quite sure how to say what she desperately wanted to talk about or how Cindy might react to some of it. Finally, she just blurted out, "He called me a slut," and once again the tears started to flow.

They sat down together, and Cindy asked, "Who called you a slut?"

"The guy that hit me."

"Who was it?"

"I don't know. It was a guy I picked up at Con Brio on Friday. Tom took me to the emergency room."

"Wait a minute. Who's Tom?"

"You know the big guy, the bouncer over at The Applegate."

"Oh, yeah. I know who you're talking about. So you met a guy after we all left on Friday night?"

"Yes. Oh, Cindy, it was just some guy I picked up. He took me to his room at the Windsor, and I was gonna fuck him, and he called me a slut, and then I tried to leave, and he hit me, and I couldn't get away."

Cindy sat there trying to take it all in.

About that time, Cindy's cell phone chimed in, and she saw that it was Brad calling. "Hey, Brad . . . Yeah, I'm with Annette. I think I should hang out here. She's, uh, not feeling too good . . . Yeah, I'll see you tomorrow.

Thanks. You're the greatest . . . I love you."

They sat for a moment, and then Annette said, "It was the worst date I ever had. I thought he was gonna kill me."

"I'm glad you're okay, Annie." Cindy squirmed in her seat a little and finally said, "Well, have you been dating anybody, or just, you know?"

Annette had her face in her hands now and just sat there for a moment. She finally looked up and said, "Do you remember that party we had on a Friday night at your folks' house when we were in high school?"

"Oh, I don't know. We had a lot of parties."

"You know that night your mom was sick? The one when Paul's friend Adam came over?"

Cindy sat there expressionless, then her eyes lit up and her hand flew up to her mouth. "You mean that time when we caught you two in the guest suite? You didn't. No, you did not!"

"Yes. Yes we did!"

"Oh my God!"

They both looked at each other, trying to read the other's expression, and then they burst out howling in laughter.

"I had no idea," Cindy said.

"Yeah, but he left me hanging," Annette said.

Annette started to reveal her secret life and to talk about some of her many escapades. Cindy sat there taken aback by it all. The only person she'd ever had sex with was Brad.

They talked into the night with complete disregard for the fact that they both had class the next morning. Cindy was all the friend Annette could ever hope for. And the healing had begun.

EIGHTEEN

Tom wasn't done with Annette. He had another piece of his plan to get out of her. He had taken a personal interest in the assaults on Annette and the other woman. It was a real-life situation that was close to home and that gave him the opportunity to apply some of the things he'd been learning in his studies at the community college. Besides, this whole business of some guy beating up on women rubbed him the wrong way.

He'd already started talking with some of the other staff there at The Applegate and was basically trying to put together some type of surveillance to monitor at least some of the comings and goings at the Windsor Inn a couple of blocks down on Applegate Street. Fortunately, there had only been two incidences so far that he knew of. Unfortunately, there had only been two incidences that he could use to develop any kind of history for fine-tuning his surveillance efforts. There wasn't any way it was going to be monitored around the clock, and the two cases had happened on different days of the week. But at least they had both happened on the weekend. They would monitor on Fridays and Saturdays, trying to catch this guy on his way in, preferably, and not on his way out.

Tom had already contacted the local police, with whom he had a bit of a rapport due to some of the 911 calls he'd made from The Applegate over the last couple of years. They had given their blessing for a neighborhood watch effort and were confident that Tom wouldn't try to do anything too heroic. Tom had always been straight up and cooperative with them. They, of course, wanted to know who the victims were. The first woman had been pretty adamant and was not willing to talk to the police. Tom wasn't too sure about Annette and said he would try to get her to cooperate.

Getting Annette to cooperate was crucial since they'd need somebody to point the proverbial finger if they were going to get the perpetrator and put him through due process. Furthermore, they needed to be able to recognize this guy, which is where Annette came in. He'd been able to get a fair amount of information out of her about what the guy looked like, but he'd not been able to talk to the other young woman. All he knew from the grapevine about her was that it had happened at the same motel on a Saturday night. He also had a graphics buddy in the criminology department at school who was willing to lend his services to do a sketch.

Annette's cell phone sounded shortly after she got home from classes Monday afternoon.

"Hey, Annette. This is Tom Garrison."

She immediately recognized his voice. "Oh, hi, Tom."

"I was wondering if I could come over at some point with my sketch artist, Joey."

"Oh, I don't know."

There was a brief pause and Tom spoke again, "Well, what's convenient for you?" Another pause. "We need to make this happen before that fool beats up somebody else. But we can work with your schedule."

She finally acquiesced, thinking in the back of her mind that it wasn't all about her, and they set up a time later in the week to get together. She was starting to find a real appreciation for Tom's efforts. He was a very busy guy and certainly had enough other things to do. She didn't know anything about the other woman, but up until recently, her relationship with Tom had only been casual. It seemed like quite an endeavor on his part for someone like her that he really didn't know, but she realized, too, that he wasn't doing it just for her. It was also about any other potential victims. She had a very positive impression of his character at that point and was glad he had gotten involved.

When they got together, Joey was cordial, but they very quickly got down to the business at hand. Within less than an hour, they had what she felt was a pretty good likeness. The thing that she came to realize, however, was that she was probably going to have to testify and identify this guy if they ever caught him. At this point she wondered why they didn't just go ahead and call the police.

The next words out of Tom's mouth were, "Is it okay

if we call the local police on this? They might already know the guy, and we might get to the bottom of it a lot quicker."

"Yes," she said.

The next question from Tom was about her willingness to testify. Again, Tom's persuasion pushed her over the edge. For someone who had impressed her as the strong silent type he was proving to have a lot more up his sleeve than she could have imagined.

Still, she expressed doubts about their effort. "You know the guy's from out of town and may never be back again?"

Tom's only response was, "That's what he'd like *you* to believe."

Tom and Joey gathered their things and took off.

*

Later that same evening, Tom was back at The Applegate working the door. The Applegate was a restaurant and bar that mostly appealed to college kids. It was a single-story brick building that sat on a corner near campus. There were plate glass windows along the front with a glass door on one side. The place was not that large and would accommodate about seventy people or so between booths, tables, and the bar. It was nothing too fancy, but it was clean and they had a roster of bands that played several nights a week. Everybody got carded when they walked in. Underage kids eighteen and older were allowed in, but only the ones old enough to drink got the plastic wristband. Tom opened the front door to The Applegate for the young man who had a mic stand in one hand and a guitar case in the other.

"Hey, thanks," he responded.

"No problem, dude," Tom said. "Nice to see you again. You guys sounded great last time."

When Jeremy came back through, Tom said, "Hey, when you're done moving your stuff, would you mind helping me out for a minute?"

Jeremy responded, "Sure."

About thirty minutes later, the two of them were on either end of a wooden bench that usually sat there on the sidewalk in front of The Applegate. Tom was explaining his surveillance plan as they moved the bench to a spot across the street from The Windsor Inn. Now his volunteers would at least have a place to sit while they kept an eye out.

When they got the bench in place, Jeremy brushed his hands together and said, "Yeah, I heard the same thing happened to this girl named Jeannie. She looked pretty beat up."

Tom immediately raised his eyebrows and wanted to know more. They talked on the way back to The Applegate. Jeremy didn't have too much more information, but it seemed clear that it was a case that had not been reported to the police, and it had happened in between the other two cases.

"Do you know what night of the week it happened?" asked Tom.

"I'm not sure," said Jeremy. "All I know is she looked fine when she was in class on Monday, and she was black and blue when I saw her at the next class on Wednesday."

That was bad news because it changed the history of events. They were no longer just looking for something to happen on a weekend. But Jeremy said he overheard something about the Windsor, so it was becoming more likely they'd find him at this location. When they got back to the bar, Tom gave Jeremy a copy of the sketch and asked if he would be able to spend a few hours a week on the surveillance. Jeremy was glad to help out as much as he could.

A few weeks later, and thus far the surveillance effort had been fruitless. Jeremy had spent a couple of evenings on the bench across the street from the Windsor. They worked in one-hour shifts because most people were too busy to spend more time than that. Unfortunately, the effort was kind of random, but they filled in the schedule the best they could with whoever was available. After several months, some of the team had dropped out. It was beginning to look like a dead end.

One night after his watch, Jeremy decided to stop in for a drink at The Applegate before heading home for bed. He ran into one of his bandmates at the bar, and pretty quickly they launched into a conversation about one of the new songs they were working on.

In the corner, not far from the bar, sat two college girls who were having a late snack and chatting. It was all Cindy could do to finally get Annette out of her apartment for anything other than school. It all seemed kind of odd to Annette. Her life was just different now. Men of all ages, shapes, and sizes continued to notice her. But she no longer had any interest. Her radar was turned off. As far as she was concerned, there was nothing coming in that she needed to pay attention to.

During a lull in her chat with Cindy, she heard a voice that got her attention, and she didn't know why. It was the sound of a male voice. Intermittently the voice sang a short phrase, and she saw two guys at the bar who were having an animated conversation. What really struck her at the moment had nothing to do with what he looked like, although there was nothing wrong with the way he looked. She didn't notice any of the things that she used to. This was a guy she might have never noticed at all. But she noticed his voice, and she knew that voice, but she couldn't quite place it.

NINETEEN

Jeremy was in his bed on his back with the sheet and covers pulled up under his chin. About three weeks ago he'd been dumped by his girlfriend. He'd finally made a connection with a very attractive girl at school. She wasn't in the music department, but he'd met her in one of his other classes. They started spending time together and going out on casual dates when they both had the free time. There had been one evening in particular midway through their relationship that they'd started to kiss. It was glorious for him. And each time after that they got a little more involved, and he got a little more aroused. He was very attracted to her and had fantasized about her several times, but they'd never actually been sexually involved beyond some lengthy kissing, holding, and touching each other. So out of the blue after about two months she told him that she was seeing someone else, and that was it.

He was pretty down about it for a while. That's when a few of his friends decided to intercede. Although he never spoke of it specifically, they suspected that he was still a virgin and felt sorry for him after being dumped by his girl. At that point, they decided to see what they could do, pooled what few spare dollars they had, and hooked Jeremy up with a fine looking redhead.

Little did they know that their attempt to cure Jeremy's virginity had failed completely. So there he was, after an embarrassing and confusing rendezvous with this beautiful girl, in his own bed all alone and very horny. It had been quite some time since his last release and his balls were literally aching. He started fantasizing about the beautiful redhead that he'd met earlier that evening, who had taken him up to her room and undressed for him. He couldn't help but be turned on by what he'd seen, even though he'd not been able to consummate the act when she was right there in front of him. So with eyes closed, picturing her in his mind, he finished what had been started.

*

Now that a new semester had begun and Annette was no longer spending her time looking for her next date, she had decided to do something different with her time. She signed up for one of the choral classes in the music department there at school. She'd passed the audition for the class and was excited about singing again.

When she attended the first class, she found her way into the alto section positioned directly in front of the basses. She remembered the choir director from her audition, Dr. Filibert. He was an imposing figure, a large white man about six feet tall or maybe six one. He was broad, without an ounce of fat, and always wore a suit. He was completely bald and looked like he should have had a monocle in one eye. They started right off sight singing, and as they were going through the first piece, she heard it again coming from right behind her. She swore it was that same voice she'd heard the other night at The Applegate. Then she realized it was also the same voice she'd heard singing in a band on another occasion at The Applegate. She was dying to know if it was the same person she'd seen the other night, but she couldn't just turn around and look at him. Something about his voice was taking her away, and she found herself just standing there with her eyes closed, listening. About that time there was the sound of a baton tapping on a music stand, and the choir came to an abrupt stop.

Her eyes flew open and Filibert was looking directly at her. "I'm glad you're so enraptured by the music, but would you care to open your mouth and make some noise along with the rest of us?"

The rest of the choir burst into a flurry of laughter.

They started the piece again from a spot just before where they'd stopped for her comedic interlude. She found her focus and was pleased that she wasn't completely confused by the written music and that some of her reading skills were still there. When the class was over, she turned to the side to exit from between the rows of chairs and glanced out of the corner of her eyes to see who it was. It was the same curly-haired young man she'd seen at the bar, and he was having a lively conversation with one of the other basses. For the first time that she could remember, she was interested in a guy, not interested in having sex with him, not interested in his dick, but interested in him. And for the first time in her life, she didn't know how to act or what to say. She paused and then walked out of the choir room.

Later in the week, she had a call from Cindy. "Hey, Annette. What are you doing tonight?"

"Oh, I need to get caught up on some homework and housework."

"Housework? Forget that! It's Friday night. Come on out with me and Brad; we're going to The Applegate, and I wanna hear all about how bad you sounded in your new choir."

"Oh, I don't think so, Cindy."

"Oh, please! There's no need for you to be a complete stick in the mud. Besides, there's a great band you should hear."

Annette finally acquiesced. Brad and Cindy met with Annette at her place, and they went together from there over to The Applegate. They found a couple of other friends at a table not too far from the bandstand and sat down with them. It was about thirty minutes before the band was due to go on. They ordered a few munchies and their banter started. So when Cindy asked Annette about her choral class, she paused, thought for a moment, and decided she'd confess her little faux pas.

She talked about the first song they sang and about the voice she'd heard from behind her. "I was just loving the sound of his voice, and I stopped singing, and I was just standing there like a goof with my eyes closed when Dr. Filibert started banging his baton on the music stand."

When she told them what the director had said, everybody at the table burst out laughing. And with one hand on the side of her face and a tear streaming down her cheek, Annette laughed out loud with them. It was a great feeling.

A moment later, she heard a voice say, "Oh, is that what happened? You were right in front of me, and I didn't know what was going on."

She turned and saw who it was. She put a hand over her mouth with a look of surprise on her face and just sat there.

Finally, she extended her hand and said, "Hi, I'm Annette."

He shook her hand, then with a beautiful deep voice and a pleasant smile on his face, he said, "Hi, I'm Jeremy."

And then he walked away and stepped onto the bandstand.

The band started playing, and Annette was mesmerized. Jeremy was totally ensconced in what he was doing, totally suspended in the moment, totally lost in the music. He was playing an acoustic guitar, but didn't sing on the first couple of songs. The leader of the band, Frankie, was an older guy in his early thirties. He had a beer belly, long unruly hair, and a gravelly voice. He played electric guitar and sang the first two songs. Midway through the next song she heard Jeremy singing a beautiful harmony part. His voice was a stark contrast to Frankie's. Later in the set, Jeremy stepped up to the mic and sang a ballad. Annette closed her eyes and was taken away by the emotion in his voice.

Moments after they finished the last song of the set, Frankie bounced down off the stage and walked right up to the table where Annette was sitting with her party.

"Oh my, my, my," he said. "What have we here, another beautiful flower in the bed." He was looking straight at Annette. "Oh please, good posture is *so* important. Shoulders back, dear."

And without even realizing it, she sat up a little taller and brought her shoulders back, which, of course, made her breasts a little more pronounced.

"Oh, yes. I knew it. You have lovely tits under that blouse you're wearing."

His salacious comment elicited a round of laughter from everyone at the table.

Then Frankie started looking around and in a louder voice said, "Why has no one introduced me to this lovely young thing before?"

Frankie was a bona fide character—a loud mouthed, happy-go-lucky social animal who cursed like a sailor and enjoyed every minute of it. He introduced himself to pretty much everybody in the place and flirted with every girl before the night was over. He could talk your ear off all night long and say nothing.

Jeremy was very interested in getting back to Annette after they'd finished playing their set. But when he saw that Frankie had dominated her table with his "performance," he paused, gave Annette a nervous glance, and then just walked over to the bar.

She saw him pass by and was disappointed that he hadn't stopped back to see her.

Later that night after the gig was over, Jeremy saw Frankie and Annette talking by the door as Annette was on her way out with Cindy and Brad. Frankie had his cell phone out punching in her number. Jeremy went back to work packing up his gear. *Oh well,* he thought.

TWENTY

The following week, Annette found herself anticipating the next choral class with delight. Not only was she enjoying singing, it was another opportunity to see Jeremy and try to connect with him. She had become quite intrigued by this young man with the beautiful voice, the passion for his music, and his reserved nature. She found herself thinking about him from time to time. That was something she had never done before. Never had she had this type of interest in someone and never had she spent time thinking about anyone like this.

She arrived at the next choral class a few minutes early and was casually scanning the choir room, but Jeremy was not there. She found her seat and started looking over the music.

About that time, Dr. Filibert started in. "Okay, people. This is *not* a sight singing class. You've got to learn the music. The performances at the end of the semester will be done from heart. There will be no sheet music in front of you!"

Jeremy arrived during the middle of the announcement and quickly took a seat with the basses behind her. He never looked her way.

By the time the class was over, she'd decided to be direct and just walk up and talk to him. She had several things in mind that she might say to try and get a conversation started. When the director dismissed them at the end of class, she immediately gathered her things and stood.

She caught up to Jeremy as he was on his way out. "Hi, Jeremy."

Before she could say anything else, he stammered, "I've got to go."

And he walked out. Annette just stood there for a moment. Had she just been snubbed? And for that moment, she was consumed with disappointment, an angst that she'd never felt. That had never happened to her before.

TWENTY-ONE

Jeremy sat alone in his room after a long day. It wasn't an apartment, just a single room with his bed, a bedside table, a chest of drawers, and a small desk and chair. In the corner was a tall cardboard box with a rack in it for hanging clothes. There was just enough space left over for his two guitars and an amp. The bath down the hall was shared with the other tenants on his floor, and the paint was peeling off the walls in the hallway.

He was in a funk. *She is so beautiful.* He pictured her face in his mind. He loved her brown eyes, the shape of her mouth. She had such a beautiful ass. *Oh my God. What a beautiful ass.* He wanted to see her, look at her, touch her. But there was something else about her. The little incident on the first day in choir made her seem . . . more human, approachable, someone he could talk to. He couldn't believe she was there at the last gig he'd played. He was so thrilled. And when he'd overheard how much she liked his voice, he was even more psyched and felt a boost of confidence that he didn't usually have. But when he'd seen the smile on her face as Frankie was getting her phone number, he was crushed. He'd decided, whether consciously or not, that she wasn't going to happen for him. He couldn't believe he just blew her off at the last choir rehearsal, but he knew it was no use.

The next day was a Saturday. Jeremy had no classes and no other commitments except for a rehearsal with the band later that afternoon. He slept in and finally decided to get up and spend some time going over the music for the rehearsal before it got too late in the day. He walked down to the coffee shop on the corner and got a breakfast sandwich and a bottle of juice. There was no one there that he knew, so he took his food back to his room and started listening to the recordings of the songs that Frankie had given him for the rehearsal. One song he'd heard before and really liked, but it was by a female artist. He was a little puzzled but decided that Frankie might be singing it in a different key.

Jeremy was taken by surprise later that day when he walked in the door with his guitars at the place where the band had rehearsals. Annette was standing there with her back to the door, her hair pulled back in a long ponytail. There she was with that beautiful ass in a pair of skin-tight jeans. She looked great, and Frankie was standing close to her with one arm draped around her waist. They were singing together the song that he'd worked on earlier. Frankie and Annette looked each other in the face as they sang together, and Jeremy just stood there for a moment with his mouth open. He finally walked in and started setting up.

After they finished the chorus of the song, Frankie spoke up. "Hey man, I hope you don't mind I invited Annette to sit in on our rehearsal. She never sang in a band before, and I told her she could hang out and sing something with us."

"Yeah, sure," Jeremy replied.

Despite his awkward feelings at the moment, he found his focus, and before long it was all about the music. He immediately recognized that Annette had a good voice and really liked the way she sounded on that tune. In the meantime, the drummer and the bass player had arrived and were ready to go. Frankie counted it off, and they started playing the song. When they got to the chorus of the song, Jeremy already had a harmony part in mind and started to sing along. Frankie stopped them midway through. He put a finger in one ear and sang a few notes by himself. Then they started again on the chorus so that Frankie could iron out the vocal part he was trying to sing. He stopped the band again.

"I don't know, man," Frankie said. "I think you guys sound great together just the two of you. I'm gonna lay out."

And so they started the song again from the chorus, Annette looking into Jeremy's face as they sang. And they sounded great together.

TWENTY-TWO

He reached down with his large hands and gently picked up his young daughter and gave her a kiss on the cheek.

"Why have you got to go, Daddy?" Susie asked.

"Well, it's a business trip, sweetie," he replied. "I've got to do it for work."

Gerald Swan was a college graduate who married his high school sweetheart and had settled into a routine with family and work. He made decent money working a nine-to-five office job—a job that, thankfully, required no travel. His wife worked part time, kept the home, and took care of their daughter. She dropped Susie off at day care on the days that she worked. She, too, had settled into a placid routine. She and Gerald were very comfortable with each other and had a quiet, conservative, and generally uneventful lifestyle. They rarely had sex, and when they did, it was always missionary style, and there had never, ever been any oral sex involved, nothing that varied from their very limited routine. They had both been virgins when they were married and their daughter, Susie, arrived about three years later.

Gerald's younger years may have seemed unremarkable,

but underneath the surface of his seemingly normal exterior a disturbed psyche was being fostered. His father spent little time with him and was aloof at best. Some of Gerald's most vivid memories of his family were the events he witnessed from the sideline. There was more than one occasion that he saw his father slapping his mother in anger.

When his father caught him looking at them from a distance, he would holler, "What are you lookin' at, boy?" which sent him running.

Gerald had no way of knowing that his mother had started an extra-marital affair at one point in his early childhood. But Gerald saw the aftermath first hand. Gerald's father had his suspicions and confronted his mother angrily. It turned into a shouting match. Gerald heard the commotion, walked down the hallway, and looked into the room just in time to see his father mercilessly beating his mother with his fists. It was an extreme image that would have an indelible impact on the young boy's character.

Gerald's wife knew nothing of his agitation, his contempt, his silent fury. He deemed sexually attractive women, flirtatious women, women who seduced a man's attention with their bodies as repugnant. But they were everywhere, making a mockery of his very nature. They were in magazines, on the TV, in restaurants, walking around the mall. As far as he was concerned, society was in a depraved state. Watching TV became increasingly distasteful for him. Sometimes in the evenings while drinking a glass of scotch, he found himself hitting the remote, going from channel to channel. Every time an attractive woman appeared who demonstrated the least bit of her sexuality, he would get angrier and change the channel. Yet he sat in silence, his eyes burning, never uttering a word.

On one of these occasions, his wife had thrown her hands up and said, "I just can't keep up with whatever it is you're trying to watch, Gerald," and with that she left the room and went to bed.

He was, however, finding much satisfaction in his outings away from home on his "business trips." It assuaged his rage greatly, at least temporarily. He'd been away from home numerous times in his attempts to seduce a beautiful, sexy, deserving woman. He was almost at wits' end before he connected that first time. He remembered it vividly; it was the night of a full moon. From there it seemed to get easier, and his punishments became more and more brutal. He was no longer concerned or frustrated if he didn't connect on a given outing, if he didn't get the opportunity to deliver his justice. He'd become more and more enraptured with the whole process, and he knew there would be another success, another deserving woman, if not that time, then the next.

He'd thought about changing the venue for his acts of justice, but the Windsor Inn never required him to present any kind of ID or address information. He just paid the cash up front and got the room key. Besides, it was the location of his first success.

He thought about his last successful outing. Oh, she was asking for it from the start. The way she was dressed, the way she looked at him. She sat there on that barstool with that round ass in those skin-tight jeans. She had looked over her shoulder at him and winked. All of them, the whole lot of those girls, needed to be punished. But when he approached the bar where they sat and began chatting, she was the one who was the most blatant in her perverse assault on his morality. She enticed him.

When they got to his room, he let her have her way with him, let that demon seal her own fate. When he defiled her mouth with his cock and she enjoyed it, he gave it to her. He was astride her torso and kept his cock deep in her throat giving her his emission. And he just kept it there deep in her throat as she began to squirm, trying to free herself. She began tapping on both of his legs with the palms of her hands as she lay there unable to move.

He then pulled himself out suddenly and just as she uttered "thank you" he slapped her across the face.

When she reached up with her hands to defend herself, he beat her, beat her with his fists, beat that slut until she was unconscious.

TWENTY-THREE

"Oh, come on, Betty! It'll be fun. You never go out with us." One of Betty's coworkers, Diane, was trying to persuade her to join a group from the office that was going out for drinks after work.

Betty was a white woman in her late twenties, with medium short blond hair that she kept neatly in place. She was not unattractive, but she was quite a wallflower. She was very conservative both in her attire and her mannerisms.

"We won't keep you out late, I promise," Diane said.

"No, no, I just couldn't," Betty responded. "I've got to pick up my daughter after work, and Gerald is out of town on one of his business trips."

"Hey, doesn't your daughter go to the same day care that my two go to?"

"Why yes, yes she does, but—"

"But, nothin'! You remember my neighbor, Catherine, don't you? Well, she's picking up my kids. I'll have her pick up Susie, too. They can hang out at Catherine's place for a couple of hours and eat pizza. It'll be great."

"Well, I don't know."

"Just give the day care a call and let them know that Catherine will be picking up Susie. I'll call Catherine."

"Well, I don't know," Betty stammered again.

At that moment, Natalie chimed in. "What is yo problem, lady? You too good to hang with yo peeps from the office? We not good enough for you?" And with that comment, all three of the women who had been trying to talk Betty into joining them burst into laughter.

Mr. Flint, the office manager, glanced over as he walked by and said, "Oh, go ahead, Betty. You need to have a little fun."

"Well, alright," she finally acquiesced.

The other three women started clapping and cheering.

Betty started to blush. "Oh my word."

Betty got in her car after work and followed the other women to the restaurant. When they arrived at their destination, they got one of the last remaining spots available in the place. The four young women sat down together at a round high-top table very close to the bar. It was full of people and noisy with the clamor of everybody talking and laughing. It was nothing like Mrs. Swan was used to, and she certainly didn't sit near the bar when she dined out.

Shortly after they got settled at their table, a waitress came and asked for their drink order.

Diane immediately spoke up. "They have got the best Baltimore Zoos at this place. Betty, you've got to have one."

"Oh, I don't know," Betty said. "I've never heard of such a thing."

"If you don't like it, we'll get you something else."

Betty acquiesced for a second time, and they ordered their drinks. Betty was not much of a drinker. She wasn't a teetotaler, but she drank alcohol very infrequently. When the drinks arrived, Diane could see that Betty was a little confused and helped her out. "Just take the little glass of beer on top and pour some of it into the big glass. It'll give it a little fizz."

Betty did as instructed and was very pleased when she tasted the drink. It didn't seem too strong going down, but it was a very stiff drink. The group of young ladies were laughing and chatting, mostly about the different personalities in the office. Then Natalie started talking about a date she had last weekend. It was a guy that she'd been out with several times and their date had started to become romantic. Natalie went on and on about how the guy had tried to put the moves on her.

"I have to give him credit," she said. "He did *not* give up easy. Uh, uh. No indeed. That joker thought he was gettin' some of dis, but it was not on *my* agenda. Then he started whispering in my ear about all he was gonna do to me, about kissin' me here and kissin' me there and how he wanted to go down on me and shit. I said, 'Wait just a minute, you don't know me that well.'"

At this point, everybody was pretty much in hysterics as Natalie continued to berate her over-enthusiastic date, everybody except Betty. She just sat there, wide eyed, taking it all in.

The Baltimore Zoo had kicked in pretty hard for Betty at this point, and she leaned over and whispered in Diane's ear, "What does she mean 'going down'?"

Diane started to snicker and leaned over to Betty's ear and whispered, "You know, oral sex. He wanted to eat her pussy."

Betty was sucking her straw, taking another gulp of the drink into her mouth. But when she heard that, her eyes flew open, and she spewed the drink out of her mouth halfway across the table. Of course, the other women had overheard their whispers and at that point they were all laughing hysterically, everybody except Betty that is.

Natalie put her hands on her hips, looked at Betty, and said, "You mean to tell me that Mr. Swan ain't never gone down on you before?"

Betty just sat there, wide eyed.

All Natalie could say next was, "Oh Lord, girl. You don't know how to live."

The merriment carried on for another hour, and there was no turning back. Everybody except Betty had stories to tell about amorous adventures. Some of the stories were pretty detailed about some very fondly remembered sexual encounters. Miranda, one of the other members of the group, had everyone, including Betty, on the edge of their seats as she spoke of a particular boyfriend who apparently had a great talent for oral sex. Betty sat there listening with rapt attention, her head swirling from the drink she had finished, becoming increasingly aroused as Miranda divulged his every delicate maneuver that was lovingly bestowed on the most private ingredient of her femininity.

As their after-work social outing was wrapping up, Betty excused herself and made her way to the ladies' room. Diane took one look at her unsteady gait and jumped up to accompany her. When they got back to the table, Diane asked Betty if she could drive her home. Betty said no and that she had to pick up Susie. Diane knew better. She told Betty not to worry, that they could pick up Susie on their way. Diane told her that she would get her the next morning so they could pick up Betty's car. Fortunately, Betty acquiesced for a third time.

After Diane dropped off Betty and Susie, Betty got Susie into bed as quickly as she could and stumbled into her own bed not long after. She lay there in her bed with her covers pulled up under her chin, thinking about the one story that Miranda had told. She imagined what it would be like, and she began to touch herself. It was something she had never done before. She had never had an orgasm before either—until that night.

TWENTY-FOUR

Betty looked nervously around the lunchroom at the office where she worked. There it was with a number of books and magazines on the table in the corner. She had noticed it before but never paid attention until now. After the evening that she had joined her coworkers for drinks, this one book took on a new interest. It was one of those self-help type of books about romancing your husband. She had idly picked it up once before, but immediately set it back down due to its graphic nature. It had startled her and even offended her then. Now she wanted to read it. She stepped into the doorway of the lunchroom, took a quick look up and down the hallway, then quickly walked over to the corner, picked up the book, and stuffed it into her purse. It was the end of her workday. She said goodbye to Mr. Flint on her way out of the office.

She decided she would keep it right there at the bottom of her purse. She figured that was as safe a place as any. Whenever she had private time around the house when Gerald was at work, she would take it out and read it. She was becoming more and more entranced with the idea of trying new things with her husband. She wanted to seduce him and turn him on and try some of the things she had read about. And she imagined some of the things he might do to her as they explored a new sexuality with each other. She was secretly thrilled.

After a couple of weeks, she finished the book and was enthused about spending time with Gerald and trying to get involved with him in a more intimate way. One evening after putting Susie to bed, she found him in his usual spot on the couch in front of the TV. She sat down on the couch and sidled up next to him, something she never did. She usually sat by herself in the chair. She lay her head on his shoulder and just enjoyed being next to him. After a few moments, she turned toward him and gave him a lingering kiss on the cheek. He glanced at her sideways and furrowed his brow, acknowledging the distraction, but then returned his gaze to the TV. At that next moment, a commercial came on with a provocative young woman in the ad. He grabbed the remote and changed the channel. Oblivious to this, she stretched out beside him on the couch and lay the side of her head on his lap facing the TV. She stayed there for a few moments enjoying the novelty of this physical interaction with him. She then reached up and placed her hand on his thigh not far from his groin. He sat there with a look of horror on his face. He had no idea what she was doing or why she was acting this way. He just sat there not knowing how to respond. She turned her head down and nuzzled his lap, feeling his penis beneath his trousers, and she started to become aroused. Suddenly she tumbled off of the couch onto the floor as he stood up, still clutching the remote in one hand.

"What are you doing?" he shouted.

"Gerald? I just wanted . . . I just wanted to be close to you," she stammered, feeling bewildered.

He walked out of the room.

Betty's attention was distracted as Susie came into the room sobbing. "I had a bad dream, Mommy."

TWENTY-FIVE

Jeremy left the rooming house where he lived with his cell phone and a folded piece of paper in his pocket. The piece of paper was a copy of the sketch, which also included a bullet list of the man's features. Jeremy had reviewed it again carefully before leaving and felt he had a pretty good idea of who he was looking for. It was a night he had committed to be on watch for an hour. He walked over to Applegate Street and popped into The Applegate and said a quick hello to Tom just to let him know he was on duty. He then walked across the street and up a couple more blocks, finally taking a seat on the bench across from the Windsor Inn. The bench was away from the curb, up against a storefront under an awning, but there was a clear view of the entrance to the motel across the street. There was the usual traffic on the street and a few people coming and going from the Windsor, but no one who remotely resembled the man he was looking for.

As he sat there lonely and bored, he began to think about Annette. He was so disappointed that she was getting involved with Frankie instead of him. He couldn't blame Frankie; she was a beautiful girl. She was talented.

She was approachable. She was someone who seemed real. And Frankie was the outgoing type who had the gift of gab and an outrageous sense of humor that made everybody laugh. He thought it was no wonder that she was interested in Frankie and not him. Jeremy's mind started in on its usual cascade of self-reproach. *If I wasn't so shy; if I had a sense of humor and could make people laugh; if I were better looking; if I were more mature; if I wasn't such an eternal fucking virgin. Chicks can smell me coming a mile away and they start running . . .*

At about that time, he heard a familiar gravelly voice, "Hey, man, I caught you in the act."

It was Frankie who had just walked up on him from the same side of the street. He had a grocery bag full of stuff in one arm. He put the bag down on the sidewalk and then sat down next to Jeremy.

"Tom over at The Applegate told me you were helping him out with his surveillance thing," Frankie said.

Jeremy sat up from the slouched position he was in and said, "Yeah, I've done this a couple of times."

"That's a beautiful philanthropic thing you're doing here, man."

"Thanks, I just hope they catch this guy before he beats somebody else up. He seems to be getting worse."

Jeremy continued scanning the other side of the street.

"Yeah, me, too. I was on my way home from the grocery store and thought I'd check in on you. Hey, that was a nice rehearsal we had the other day. How about Annette, man? She can sing."

"Yeah, I thought she sounded great."

"I thought the two of you sounded great."

"So, are you going to be taking her out?"

"Say what?" Frankie replied in a surprised tone.

"I mean, I thought you two were seeing each other. You know?"

"Dude, are you shittin' me? Sabrina would cut my *balls* off!"

"Sabrina?"

"Yeah, Sabrina. She's my ol' lady. Dude, I'm sorry. I thought you knew I was married."

Jeremy looked at him in complete surprise, and Frankie continued. "Shit, I flirt with everybody. That don't mean nothin'. Sabrina and I been married for six years. We got a seven-year-old kid together. I'm telling you, man, it's bliss, happy family and everything."

Jeremy just sat there in disbelief.

"Besides," Frankie continued, "when she came into the rehearsal, the only thing she could talk about was you. You got your cell phone?"

Jeremy pulled the cell phone out of his pocket.

"Here, put her number in your contact list." Frankie got out his cell phone, found Annette's number, and read it out loud for Jeremy.

After they said good night, Frankie picked up his grocery bag and continued on his way home. Jeremy sat there with a sense of relief. He was almost ebullient. He had a tremendous sense of hope, and he was so amused by the whole scenario with Frankie, a happily married man who also happened to be an incorrigible flirt.

He was dying to call Annette.

After the next person on the watch shift arrived, Jeremy jogged toward home. He stopped into the coffee shop on the corner, used their restroom, bought something to drink, and ran up to his room. Without stopping to think about it, he found her name in the contact list on his cell phone and hit the send button.

Annette answered, "Hello."

"Hi, is this Annette?"

She immediately recognized his voice. "Hi, Jeremy."

He froze for a moment, not sure what to say next, but she took up the slack. "Hey, I really enjoyed the rehearsal with you guys the other day."

"Thanks, you sounded great. I mean, I really enjoyed singing with you."

"Oh, it was amazing. I've never sung with a band before."

"Hey, I want to apologize if I was kind of weird before." He paused. "You know, I thought you and Frankie might be going out or something. I just found out that he's actually married."

She laughed. "Oh jeez, he's not my type." She paused. "Jeez, I'm not sure what my type is anymore." She closed her eyes and furrowed her brow, wishing she hadn't made that last statement.

Jeremy filled the silence. "Yeah, I think he's just a big flirt. He's quite a character."

"Yes, he is," she chimed in. "Very entertaining, but not my type."

"Hey, I'm sorry," he said. "I guess it's getting kind of late. I didn't mean to keep you up or anything."

"No, no, not at all. I was just finishing up some reading for a class. Honestly, I was getting kind of tired of it anyway. So, how's the choir thing going for you? Have you got all the music memorized yet?"

And so their conversation flowed with ease. They began to get to know each other a little more, easily moving from one topic to another. And they revealed the history of themselves to each other, at least in part, talking about their childhoods and sharing many of their experiences.

Annette told him that she had dated a number of guys over the years, but no one that she really wanted to stay involved with. She did not mention her most recent "date." She didn't go there. She didn't mention anything about her former fascination, about her black dog. Jeremy confessed that he had not dated too much, but did not mention that he was still a virgin.

They were both enchanted in their conversation with each other. There was no touching or kissing or sensual pleasure that they shared that night. They weren't even in the same room together. But they were falling. And they talked for hours into the night.

TWENTY-SIX

The choir was in the middle of another rehearsal late in the semester. They stopped singing abruptly to the sound of the baton hitting the music stand.

Dr. Filibert announced loudly to the class, "Well, congratulations to Jeremy and Annette. They appear to be the only two people singing this piece without the aid of the music notation. We will not have music notation at the upcoming concert, people."

Jeremy and Annette each smiled, each pleased that the other had memorized the music.

The choir director started up again. "Okay, everybody. Take all of the music off of the stands and push the stands down. Push the top of the stand over."

Everyone did as requested. He started the piece again, his hand moving the baton gracefully through the air. Midway through you could see his brow furrow as he closed his eyes briefly and shook his head.

Directly after the rehearsal was over, Jeremy and Annette found each other.

Jeremy said "Hi" and Annette chimed in, and before she even realized what she was saying, asked, "You want to come over?"

"Yes, I'm free tonight," he said.

"Uh, great," she stammered. "Maybe we can fix something to eat."

When they got to her apartment and walked in, she realized that she hadn't picked up any groceries lately and there was nothing for them to eat.

"Oh wow," he exclaimed, "this is great."

"It's just a one-bedroom apartment," she said.

"Yeah, but you've got a kitchen," he said with great enthusiasm.

"Well," she said, "I have a confession to make. I don't think there's anything here to eat."

Jeremy chuckled, and they decided to walk down together to the nearby market and pick a few things up for dinner. On the way, they agreed that they would have spaghetti and salad.

When they arrived, Annette said, "I don't know, they don't carry my favorite sauce here."

Jeremy looked at her, smiled, and said with a mock accent, "We don't need no stinking sauce in a jar."

And Jeremy was off through the market like a man on a mission, with Annette following behind.

"I miss cooking," he said. "I used to hang out with my mom in the kitchen when I was younger. I picked up all kinds of stuff helping her cook."

He stopped in front of a display rack in the produce section, held out his arms, and exclaimed, "Tomatoes!"

Annette giggled, and he asked, "What kind of tomatoes do you like?"

"Du-uh, the *red* ones!" she said.

They were just having fun together, and before they were through, Annette wondered how many times she had been to that market in the last couple of years since she started college. A hundred times? She'd always been in a hurry, always been preoccupied with other thoughts. This was a whole new experience, an adventure.

They got back to her apartment, each with a bag of groceries in their arms.

Jeremy put his bag down on one of the counters, rubbed his hands together, started looking around, and exclaimed, "Okay! I think we're looking pretty good here. The dishwasher is empty. The trash bin is right there, and it's not too full. The counter tops and the stove are clean. I think we can stage the event."

"Stage the event?" she asked.

"Yes, stage the event. There are several things you have to do in preparation. One is for the kitchen to be clean and organized, which it is. You can't start your art without a clean canvas. Next, you gotta have all of the ingredients, which we have." He pointed at the grocery bags on the counter. "Now we get out all of the utensils, pots, skillets, and whatever that we need. Then we get all our ingredients, food, spices, everything on the countertops where we need them. Then the magic begins!" He laughed.

Annette was enjoying the whole process, enjoying his

sense of humor, his sense of organization, and his child-like enthusiasm.

"Now," he said next, "can I trust you to be the program director?" She looked at him warily. "Yes, program director," he said. "Let's get some music up in the air."

"Great idea!" she exclaimed. "I'm your program director."

She ran off to the living room, hooked up her iPod, and started some music.

Then she heard Jeremy say, "That's great, Annette, just a little louder."

She turned up the volume, returned to the kitchen, poured two glasses of wine, and they prepared their meal together.

These were all experiences she'd never shared with a guy, and she was having the time of her life. She started thinking that this whole boyfriend thing was pretty great. She paused. *Boyfriend? I've never even kissed the guy.*

After the meal, the events of a busy day had taken their toll on each of them. Annette followed Jeremy into the living room. He kicked his shoes off, then climbed onto the sofa and lay down on his side, looking at Annette with a soft smile. She nestled down on her side and spooned with him. He wrapped an arm around her and held her, his groin pressed against her backside, the scent of her hair filling his head, and their bare feet touching. He was aroused by her beauty, by her presence. He felt her with his body and just held her. He wasn't worried about getting laid. The thought that he was a virgin did not cross his mind. He was just caught up in that moment, as it was, with her. They fell asleep together.

TWENTY-SEVEN

It had been several weeks since Jeremy and Annette had shared the meal together at her place that night after choir rehearsal. They were each pretty busy and hadn't had much time to spend together, but they talked almost every day. They either saw each other in the choral class or they talked on the phone. Jeremy had wanted to take Annette out on a proper date and so they had agreed on a day and time. They were both stoked about seeing each other.

The evening of their date, shortly before Jeremy was due to arrive, Annette had a call from her mom. The elderly neighbor of her parents, Mrs. Baker, had been moved into a nursing home some time ago.

"Hey, sweetie, I've got bad news for you about Mrs. Baker."

Annette immediately assumed the worst and exclaimed, "Oh no!"

"She's still with us, but your dad and I stopped by the nursing home today. She's bedridden now."

"Is she going to be okay?"

"Well, she's getting hospice care now. It was very weird,

Annette. I mean, she usually perks up when guests come in. I mean, she always enjoyed seeing me and your dad whenever we visited, and she always asks about you. But this was different. I'm not sure she knew who we were. I just don't think she's going to be with us too much longer."

Annette did not respond. She just sat there in a state of distress.

Her mom continued. "I think you should come, Annette."

"Okay, I'll leave first thing in the morning."

"No. I think that may be too late. I mean, I just don't know. I talked with the nurse about it and she said they just have no way of knowing. She might live another week or more, but likely not."

Annette's next response was, "I'm on my way."

Annette was so consumed by the news about Mrs. Baker that she forgot about her date with Jeremy. She got her suitcase and got packed for an overnight stay. Just as she was getting ready to leave, the doorbell rang. *Oh no! I totally forgot.*

"Jeremy, I'm so sorry. Something's come up. I'm on my way to my parents' house. I'll call you in a few minutes."

With that, she picked up her suitcase and scurried out of the door, leaving Jeremy standing there looking completely bewildered.

The first thing she had to do was stop for gas. She was upset about Mrs. Baker. She was also upset about canceling her date with Jeremy at the last moment and hoped he would understand. After she finished pumping gas and got on the road, she finally called Jeremy on her cell phone.

"What's up, Annette?"

"Hey, Jeremy. I'm so sorry. Did I ever tell you about Mrs. Baker?"

"No, I don't think so."

"She was a neighbor of ours at home, an older woman. She used to babysit for me when I was a kid. Anyway, we were pretty close. She's in a nursing home now, and my mom called." Annette started to weep. "My mom says she doesn't think she's going to be with us too much longer. I may never see her again."

Jeremy's immediate response was, "Annette, I'm so sorry. When did you find out?"

"My mom called just before you came . . . I'm sorry, I know we were supposed to have a date tonight."

Jeremy interrupted her apology. "Oh, no. Forget it. You're doing the right thing. I'm so glad you're going to see her."

Annette was relieved and her heart was warmed by Jeremy's response. "Thank you," she said. "Thanks for being supportive."

"No problem. Please call me later on, after you get to see Mrs. Baker. Let me know how you're doing."

"Okay, Jeremy. Thanks. I'll talk to you later tonight."

Several minutes later after finishing her conversation

with Jeremy, she was approaching an intersection a few blocks before the interchange for the interstate. *No!* she thought. She had a green light but there it was. Without even thinking about it, she had already slammed her foot onto the brake pedal and could feel the vibration of the ABS. The car had come through the intersection right in front of her, and it was too late to stop. She could see it happening; she was going to hit that other car and was helpless to prevent it. The clamorous sound of the impact was unbelievable as she felt the seat belt clutching her in place. She'd never been in an accident before. Fortunately, she was at least able to slow down a bit and wasn't going that fast when she hit the other car. The air bag didn't deploy. After a few moments, she decided that she better get out of the intersection before someone else ran into her. She moved her car to the side of the road on the other side of the intersection and put on her flashers. But she heard something scraping when she drove that short distance. As soon as she collected her wits, she found her cell phone and called 911. At about that moment, the other driver appeared at her window and wanted to know if she was okay. She was shaken up but uninjured. The seat belt had held her in place. The other driver was fine, too, and fortunately admitted that they hadn't seen the light. The police arrived after about five minutes. The whole process seemed to take forever. The front end of Annette's car was pretty banged up, and they decided to call a tow truck. She got all of the information on the other driver, including the name and phone number of their insurance company.

So there she was. Stranded. She was on her way to her hometown to see Mrs. Baker, and she had no way to get there. It was going to be a long trip for her mom or dad to come get her and then drive all the way back. Not to mention they'd have to bring her back to school sometime later in the weekend. She called Cindy but didn't get an answer. She called a couple of other people but again didn't get an answer.

She finally decided to call Jeremy. "Hey, Jeremy."

"Annette," Jeremy answered with surprise. "I didn't expect to hear from you this soon."

"Hey, I've decided," she said. "We're going to have our date tonight after all. Do you like nursing homes?"

There was a brief pause and Jeremy said, "You know, I used to love going out to the movies, but ever since I discovered nursing homes, that's all I do."

"Great," Annette replied. "Actually, I had a wreck on my way out of town."

"Are you serious? Are you okay?"

"Yeah, I'm fine. Another driver ran a red light, and I hit them on my way into the intersection. They've called a tow truck for my car. It's pretty banged up. Hey, I'm serious. You wanna go to the nursing home?"

"Well, I already had plans for the evening, but my date kind of stood me up, so . . . yeah. Sure. Actually, I've got a gig tomorrow night. As long as we're back by noon or so it'll be fine."

"Oh, that's great Jeremy. I'll call my mom and let her know that you're coming. I'm sure that'll be fine. I'm on Radford Street, just a couple of blocks before the interstate ramp."

"Okay, let me throw some stuff in a bag, and I'll see you soon."

Annette called her mom in the meantime and let her know everything that had happened. Her mom was mainly relieved that Annette was alright. She was, however, also curious to meet Jeremy whom she'd not yet heard about.

"So . . ." her mom asked somewhat tentatively, "will he be staying with you, I mean, you know?"

"Oh jeez, Mom! Honestly, I've never even kissed the guy."

"Oh, I'm sorry. So he's just a friend."

"Well . . . no. I mean, I'm actually crazy about him, but we're just not there yet. I mean, I guess we're still kinda new."

"Okay. Well, I'll set him up in the guest room."

"Great, thanks, Mom." At about that moment, Jeremy arrived. So they were off together in his car to make the drive to her hometown to visit with Annette's dear old neighbor. They talked for the entire trip, and Annette told Jeremy all about Mrs. Baker.

TWENTY-EIGHT

Jeremy was a little anxious about their trip together. He was actually thrilled to be with Annette, but he wasn't quite sure about meeting her parents, partly because he and Annette were still sort of new, and it just seemed awkward to him. He didn't know if he was just a friend helping out, or whether he was supposed to be her boyfriend, or exactly what they were. Secondly, he wasn't sure how they'd feel about him being a musician. He was soon to discover what it was really about.

Jeremy and Annette drove straight to the nursing home. They walked in together, signed the guest register at the front desk, and then found their way to Mrs. Baker's room. Along the way were patients in wheelchairs at various points in the halls. Most of them seemed unresponsive. Many of them were in awkward positions with corrupted postures, leaning to one side or slumped over. Occasionally one would glance up with an imploring look. They found Mrs. Baker's room, and Annette rapped lightly on the door as she walked in. Jeremy followed and stood in the background. There she was on her back in the bed with her eyes squeezed closed, an expression of anguish on her face. Annette called her name softly from across the room, and she did not respond. She walked to her bedside, placed her hands on the safety rail, and called her name again softly, but again there was no response. Annette could see that she was breathing. Every once in a while, the old woman would gasp and suck in air. Sometimes she would cry out something unintelligible. Her eyes fluttered open at one point, but they did not appear to see. It was a very distressing sight. It was nothing that Annette could have expected. It was nothing she'd ever seen before. Annette just stood next to her bed realizing that it was her deathbed, acknowledging that this woman would soon pass from this life. In that moment, Annette was transformed. The sight of this dying woman was a most beautiful and poignant vision. Annette didn't want to cry, to be sad, to impose her grief. She looked at this old woman whom she had known for so many years, who had been a part of her childhood, and understood that she just was. She was whoever she was at this juncture, at this moment. Annette looked at the familiar face creased with deep lines, the auburn and gray hair, and thought how beautiful she was at that very moment, just as she was. Annette lowered the safety railing on the side of the bed and gently she lay down next to her. She propped herself up on one elbow and touched the old woman's hair, gently stroking her weathered old face. Her skin was so soft.

She whispered, "It's Annette, Mrs. Baker."

Annette stayed there on the bed just to be with her and to touch her. She placed her fingertips on the old woman's forehead and massaged her gently to relieve the stress in her face.

"I love you, Mrs. Baker."

The old woman's eyes fluttered open, and she looked directly into Annette's eyes. There it was. So dim, yet there it was. The light. And the old woman arched her back ever so slightly and her face seemed to be lifted with the expression of a child, the faintest smile upon her lips. Tears came to Annette's eyes as she smiled and beamed back down at her beloved old neighbor.

"I love you, Mrs. Baker."

They stayed for some time. Later, when Mrs. Baker's son arrived, Annette decided it would be a good time to leave. She introduced Jeremy, and they talked briefly. They said goodnight and then drove over to Annette's parent's home. When they arrived, they were warmly greeted by Annette's mother and father. Jeremy was so taken by the scene at the nursing home that whatever concerns he had previously about his situation with Annette and meeting her parents seemed inconsequential.

"Jeremy!" Mrs. Brennan announced as they came in the front door. "So nice to meet you. I'm really glad you could help Annette and get her to the nursing home to see Mrs. Baker."

"No problem, no problem at all. I was glad to do it," was Jeremy's reply.

"Hi, Jeremy. Jim Brennan," was Annette's father's introduction as he shook hands with Jeremy.

"Have you guys eaten yet?" was Mrs. Brennan's next question.

They had not, so they were welcomed into the kitchen and they gathered around the table to get acquainted.

Annette's mom asked, "How was Flossie?"

"Oh, Mom . . ." Annette paused. "You know, she was so beautiful."

Her mother looked at her quizzically as she was moving about the kitchen preparing something for them to eat. "You mean, she used to be beautiful?"

"No, I mean she *was*. I know she's dying. But you know it's what she is, it's what she's going through. And I didn't want to just be all sad about it. I guess I just had to accept her in that moment."

Jeremy nodded in understanding and recognition of her feelings.

"Oh, Annette," her mother said softly. "I guess I just never thought of it that way."

There was a moment of silent understanding as Mrs. Brennan finished preparing the food.

"Anyway," Annette continued, "I'm glad I came. Thanks for calling me. I'm glad I got to see her one more time. Her son came in before Jeremy and I left."

Annette's dad finally chimed in to change the subject. "So, I understand you had an accident today."

"Dad, it happened so fast, I couldn't believe it. I mean,

there was no way out of it. The guy came through a red light and I just ran right into him."

"But, nobody was hurt?"

"Nobody was hurt."

"Thank God for that. That's the most important thing."

They continued to chat, and finally Annette's dad spoke to Jeremy. "So, what are you into, Jeremy? I mean, what are you taking at school?"

"I'm a musician, sir."

"No way! That's fantastic. What do you play?"

"I play guitar, and I'm also a vocalist."

Annette interjected, "He's a great singer."

And so, the conversation flowed with ease. Jeremy was relieved—pleased actually—that Annette's parents were both enthused about him being a musician. Not once did anyone ask what he was really going to do for a living, which was often the case.

They finished eating and Jeremy helped Mrs. Brennan clean up the kitchen. It had gotten late and before too much longer, as the conversation wound down, Annette's mom showed Jeremy to the guest room, and everyone was off to bed.

Annette's mom had a call the next morning from Mrs. Baker's son. Flossie Baker had passed.

TWENTY-NINE

Annette and Jeremy decided the next day on their way back that they still owed each other a proper date. But it would have to wait another couple of weeks. The following weekend Annette would be going back home to attend Mrs. Baker's funeral. So they made plans once again for another day and time for their first official date.

That following Friday, Annette was able to borrow Cindy's car for the trip home since hers was still in the body shop. It seemed like a long trip by herself. She missed Jeremy's company. She thought about him as she drove. She was impressed with him. She liked that he had a passion and knew what he was doing with his life. She liked that he was willing to accompany her to the nursing home last weekend and to be a part of whatever she was going through. There were other things about him she noticed, that he helped her mom clean up the kitchen, that he knew how to cook, and that he just seemed to be such a nice guy. And, yes, he was cute. She thought he was really cute, but there was so much more. She started to become sad wishing Mrs. Baker were still alive, just so she could tell her all about Jeremy. She missed that connection, one that she'd known for so many years. She would miss Flossie Baker.

The next day Annette got up early so she'd have plenty of time to get dressed for the funeral service at Mrs. Baker's old church. She had bought a new suit earlier in the week for the occasion. It was a black and white tweed skirt and jacket that she paired with a black blouse and black pumps.

She was pretty much dressed and ready to go when she made it down to the kitchen. Her mom and dad were there having coffee and a light breakfast.

"Oh, Annette. You look great; nice suit," was her mom's first remark when she walked in.

"Thanks, Mom."

She got a little something to eat, and before long the three of them left together for the church. They arrived a little early for the family gathering in the church library before the service. Annette and her parents spoke with Mrs. Baker's two sons and daughter and their families. A little later as they filed into the front of the sanctuary with the family, a steady stream of people was coming in from the entrance at the rear. Annette sat down with her mom and dad near the front of the church in the pew behind Mrs. Baker's family. Several minutes later, she looked around to see that there was not an empty seat to be found and a number of people were standing against the back wall. The sound of a hymn being played on the pipe organ resonated up in the sanctuary as people spoke in murmurs and held on to stoic faces.

The pastor was an older man who had known Flossie Baker for many years.

"You know," he said during his eulogy, "she was no wallflower, nor was she one to leave words unsaid. If she felt there was an issue, she'd let you know." He paused. "But don't ask me how I know that."

A flurry of laughter erupted in the church, and everyone, including Annette, was either laughing or crying throughout the eulogy.

The interment came directly after the service there on the church grounds. Afterwards, everyone gathered back in the fellowship hall of the church. Annette saw quite a few people that she knew and many more that she didn't. There was quite a spread of food that was enjoyed. The sound of laughter and spirited conversation was all around as people were chatting, telling stories, and getting reacquainted.

Two young men in their early twenties were standing together talking at the far end of one of the food tables away from the crowd.

One spoke to the other in a hushed tone. "Did you see the chick with the long brown hair in the black and white suit?"

The other young man shook his head and the first one glanced and nodded his head in Annette's direction.

"She looks great," he continued. "I'd love to get her number."

The other young man looked over at Annette, then grabbed his arm, and they turned away as he spoke into his ear. "I know her, man. She used to make it with college guys when she was in high school."

"Really?"

"Yeah, I knew a guy that said she gave great head."

The young man's face lit up upon hearing this.

Annette just happened to walk up behind them on her way to get a plate of food when he spoke again. "You don't want to mess with her. She's just a slut."

They turned back around and were surprised to be face-to-face with Annette, who happened to be standing right there at that moment. She stood without expression.

One of them said, "Excuse me."

And they walked away.

*

The day finally came for their date, and Annette was looking through her closet with clothing strewn around the bedroom when she finally sat down and buried her face in her hands. *Oh jeez. What do I wear?* She had nothing that she liked for this date. He'd told her not to worry, that she didn't need to wear anything too fancy, but he wouldn't tell her where they were going. She didn't necessarily want to wear the same things she always wore to classes, and she didn't want to wear any of the clothes she used to wear when she was out on a "date." She just didn't want to look too provocative. She wouldn't let the S-word in. She did not let that word into her mind.

She finally decided on a pair of jeans, the same ones she'd worn to the rehearsal she had attended with Jeremy's band. *Are they too tight, too over the top?* she wondered. *Oh hell,* she decided. *It's just a pair of jeans.*

It was only a couple minutes after the hour when her doorbell rang at her apartment. She had unlocked the door a little earlier in anticipation of his arrival.

"Who is it?" she asked.

"The bogeyman," he replied.

She immediately recognized his voice and hollered, "Come on in!"

He opened the door, came through, and stood. She finished putting away the clothes that had been strewn about and then walked out of the bedroom. She paused, put her hands on her hips, and just looked at him. She liked him. He was cute. He had nice facial features, his curly hair always looked great, and he had the most beautiful smile on his face at that moment. She walked forward, grabbed her purse with one hand, grabbed his hand with the other, and out the door they went.

They got into his old car, jabbering away.

"Okay," she said. "Where are you taking me?"

"You'll find out soon enough," he said. "It's a place I've heard about. They're supposed to have great food, and I've never been."

They continued chatting away as he drove, enjoying

each other's company.

As he turned into the parking lot, she felt a wave of dread come over her. *Oh my God. Oh my God, please, no.* They had arrived at Ristorante Con Brio.

He smiled, unaware of her distress. "Isn't this a great looking place? Hope you don't mind that we're having Italian."

She sat there, frozen for a moment, then said, "No, no, this is great."

They got out of the car and walked up the sidewalk to the restaurant. He opened the door for her, and she walked in, her stomach in knots and her mind racing through the times she had been there before. As she walked in, she tried not to notice, but she saw the same bartender standing there behind the bar out of the corner of her eye. He was the same bartender she had made love to, and all of the events of that night came spilling back into her mind. He smiled and winked at her. She returned a brief weak smile and hoped that Jeremy had not noticed.

They met the hostess and she asked if they had reservations. Annette hoped upon hope that he had not made reservations and that they'd be too busy, that they would leave and go someplace else, anyplace else.

He replied, "Yes, party of two for Reynolds."

"Right this way," she responded as she picked up two menus and led them to their table.

They sat down, and Jeremy looked over the menu

eagerly.

"You know, I've been here before," Annette said, trying to regain a sense of composure.

"Oh, how was it?" he said.

"It was good," she said. "Me and a couple of friends of mine brought Cindy here for her birthday."

He continued looking over the menu, and her mind raced. It wasn't just spilling memories into her conscious. Now it was a deluge! She remembered the night she had come here late and picked up the bartender. She remembered the night she had picked up the well-dressed businessman from out of town. And the word came back, back into her mind with a vengeance. She felt like used goods, like something cheap that you'd buy from a second-hand store. She didn't want to be there. She didn't want to be herself, whoever she was. Jeremy deserved better. He deserved better than a slut! *Slut! Fucking slut!* She sat there with the most horrified look on her face. Jeremy looked up at her and saw it.

"What's wrong, Annette?"

She stood up. "I'm sorry. I'll be right back."

She left for the women's room. *Thank God.* There was no one else there. She just stood leaning forward with her hands on the sink counter and her eyes squeezed shut. *Breathe, just breathe. It'll be okay.* She finally relaxed her face, took a few more deep breaths, and tried to regain some composure. She washed her hands, dried them, and returned. She didn't know what to tell Jeremy.

"You okay?" he said when she got back.

"Yeah, fine," she lied. "My stomach was feeling kind of weird." Which was the truth. "I'll be okay." Another lie.

When they ordered, she got only a small salad. She kept her own internal wolves at bay well enough to get through the meal, but she could see that Jeremy was concerned, and their interaction was stifled at that point. When they left the restaurant, it had gotten kind of awkward, and Jeremy's mood, understandably, was not the same. He actually had further plans for their evening, but she told him it might be best if he took her home.

They returned to her apartment, and Jeremy escorted her from the car. She turned to face him when they got to the front door of her apartment.

"Hey, I'm sorry you're not feeling good," he said.

"I'll be okay. I've just got too much on my mind."

Jeremy looked at her quizzically, then looked down. She grabbed his shirt with one hand to get his attention and looked him in the eye.

"It's not you. It's not you," she said.

Looking at each other, they froze in that moment with their faces close together. He felt her breath as she exhaled. Still looking into each other's eyes, he exhaled and waited, suspended in that moment, waiting for her to breathe again. She exhaled and he breathed in, breathed in her sweet warm breath. It was an intoxicating experience he'd never had. He finally leaned in slowly to kiss her, to kiss that beautiful mouth, to kiss the breath of this beautiful woman that he was falling in love with. She turned her head.

She began to cry, ran into her apartment, and closed the door behind her.

THIRTY

Betty wondered what had happened that night she tried to get closer to Gerald, that night she tried to express her sexuality with him. She was confused and ran several scenarios through her mind trying to resolve the event. But she had been distracted by Susie's nightmare. Gerald never spoke of it, and she was reluctant to ask him about it. She finally decided that the timing had been wrong, and that maybe he had just had a hard day at work. But she still had the prospect on her mind. She still wanted to be involved with him, to seduce him, and to find her sexuality with him.

There had been another occasion since that first one. Another glorious event on an evening in bed alone. She had been looking over certain portions of her secret book again and started to become aroused. She closed her eyes and began to fantasize about Gerald. She pictured herself on the bed with a skirt on. He slowly lifted her skirt to reveal her. She had no panties on. He looked down at her pubic hair, and she parted her legs.

He whispered her name lovingly, "Oh, Betty."

He got down on his knees and lowered his face,

lowered his face down onto her most private place. He put his mouth on her pussy. As she imagined the details in her mind, she touched herself. She felt her own nipples as she was lost in her fantasy, becoming more and more aroused. She placed her hand between her legs and pushed her middle finger into her wet pussy. She found her rhythm and took herself to the brink, savoring the sensation until she couldn't help herself, and it happened again.

The next day she decided to take Susie into daycare a couple of hours early and stopped by the mall before going to work. With the encouragement of her friends from work, she had decided it was time for some new clothes, something a little more provocative that she could wear for Gerald. She stopped by a couple of places and was pleased to find some things she thought she looked good in without being too far out of her norm. She had been undecided about a particular skirt.

When she tried it on, she commented to the young lady that was helping her. "I don't know. I think this is too short."

The sales clerk shot back, "Oh, you've got nice legs. That's definitely working for you. I'd get that one if I were you."

So she got the skirt along with a couple of other items.

She made arrangements for Susie to spend time at a friend's house on Saturday afternoon so she could have some relaxed time with Gerald. After dropping Susie off, she snuck into the bedroom and put on some of her new clothes, including the skirt. Gerald was in the dining room at the table just finishing up some paperwork he'd been working on. She walked in and immediately got his attention.

"Can I get you something to drink?" she asked with a smile on her face and her hand on his shoulder.

"Yeah, that would be fine," he responded.

She turned to walk into the kitchen as he stared at her. Not only were her legs on display, but the tight skirt showed off her derriere just as well.

"How about a beer?" she asked.

"Yes."

He couldn't believe what he was seeing. She had never come on to him before. Never. He kept his cool for the moment, his eyes burning with the intensity of his reaction. *His own wife. His own wife!* He realized that she had fallen prey to the same depravity as the rest of the world. *She's trying to seduce me. What has happened to her?* She came back in, handed him the beer and stood close to him, her bare leg touching his elbow. He sat there stone cold. He decided he had to let her. He was going to let her . . . She started rubbing the top of his head with her fingers and pressed herself closer to him. She had no panties on. She lifted her skirt with her eyes closed and exposed herself to him. And she waited in that breathtaking moment, giving herself to him. He stood up and pulled his pants and underwear off, exposing his now erect penis.

"Is this what you want?" he said.

"Yes," she replied.

He took her by the shoulders and sat her in the chair. Then he placed the tip of his hard dick to her lips. She closed her eyes. Unknowingly, she sealed her own fate. She took him into her mouth. She caressed his hard dick with her mouth and with her tongue. She was enraptured with this whole new experience, and he came in her mouth. She looked up at him lovingly just as he pulled himself out and slapped her across the face. She screamed in complete shock and surprise. She saw him pulling his fist back. It was the last thing she remembered.

THIRTY-ONE

Betty heard the sound of her cell phone. She lay on her side in a heap on the dining room floor. The left side of her face was in pain.

She got up and retrieved her phone from the counter in the kitchen. "Hello."

"Hey, Betty. This is Jan. Just wondering when you were picking up Susie."

Betty was supposed to have picked up Susie at four o'clock and it was going on five.

"Oh, I'm so sorry, Jan . . . I must have fallen asleep. I'll be there very shortly."

"Oh, that's fine. We'll see you soon."

Betty was in a fog. She went into the master suite, brushed her teeth, cleaned up the one cheek that had been bleeding, and changed her clothes. Gerald was gone.

When she got to Jan's house, Susie came running down the sidewalk to greet her and immediately exclaimed, "What happened to your face, Mommy?"

Jan and her daughter had come out as well. Jan took a look, winced, and said "Oh, that's a nasty one."

Betty just stood there for a moment with Susie in

her arms and finally stammered, "Oh, it was just a silly accident."

Gerald was still out when she put Susie to bed later that evening. She sat on the chair in the living room in silence with her mind in turmoil. She sat there trying to make sense of what had happened. She felt so alone and so confused. She felt guilty. She felt it was wrong to have ever picked up that book. It was wrong to dress the way she did and to act the way she acted with Gerald. She sat there, her mind in darkness. *Was it wrong? Is everyone who ever read that book wrong? Were my girlfriends at the office a bad influence? Is it a sin to want to enjoy your sexuality with your own husband?* All of these thoughts were tumbling in her mind, yet there was another inescapable, nagging realization that she did not face. At that moment the front door opened, and Gerald came in.

*

Betty went to work as usual on Monday afternoon hoping that no one would notice or comment on the bruises— the bruises on her face that she had tried to cover with make-up. Her workday was pretty uneventful until she met Diane later that afternoon in the ladies' room.

"What happened to your face, Betty?"

"Oh, it was just a silly accident," Betty said.

"Oh, please. Don't bullshit me."

"I'm sorry," Betty said indignantly. "I'm not accustomed

to being spoken to in that manner." She turned to leave.

"Oh, but it's okay to let somebody pound you in the face?"

The words hung in the air, and Betty froze.

She finally reached for the door handle to leave, and Diane spoke again, "Betty, think about Susie." Betty froze again and Diane continued, "That looks like a nine-one-one call to me, Betty. And even if you're fool enough to let him do this to you, you don't want Susie living in this situation. You do *not* want Susie growing up with this."

Betty finally turned and faced Diane. She looked up briefly, then cast her eyes down and said softly, "Thank you, Diane."

THIRTY-TWO

Tom stood with his hands behind his back, one clasping the other, looking out the window of his bedroom, his face illuminated by the light of the moon. He was preoccupied. Savannah was in the bathroom brushing her teeth. It was getting late, and she was tired. When she was done, she flipped out the light and climbed into bed.

"C'mon, Tom, it's time for bed," she murmured.

Tom barely heard her, but lay down beside her, his train of thought still going. He was disappointed. After several months, there was nothing to show for his efforts to find the guy who had beaten Annette. Even more upsetting was the recent news that there had been another victim. That brought the count to four that he knew of. The last one had experienced much more severe injuries than Annette—although the psychological injuries were perhaps the most egregious result of the assaults. He racked his brain, reviewing what he knew about the cases. He had talked to the police in the meantime, who were still making their own efforts, but unfortunately, they had nothing new to add. His mind was methodical, thinking in turn about every victim, what he knew about each of their cases, and he tried to remember what Annette had told him, tried to remember everything about that night and everything she might have said. Was there something he was missing, anything that might put his efforts in a different direction?

At that moment, Savannah turned in the bed and said, "Close the blinds, Tom, that moon is too bright."

He suddenly sat bolt upright in the bed, his eyebrows raised and his eyes wide open.

The next day Tom was on and off the phone whenever he got the chance. He already knew the date for two of the cases, including the night that Annette had been beaten, but he didn't know the dates of all of them. He was able to determine the date for one more of the cases. The next chance he got later in the day he sat down at the computer and started looking for lunar information. He entered all of the dates in turn to determine the phase of the moon for each. *Bingo!* He had remembered the night in the emergency room with Annette, and the guy that spewed his cookies and then fell on his face. He remembered an older woman, one of the medical staff that ran over to assist. She had said, "These things always happen on a full moon." Indeed, three of the attacks had all happened on the night of a full moon.

Next, he entered yesterday's date. It had been a bright moon, but he didn't know if it had been full. He determined that tomorrow night would be the next full moon. *Damn it!* he thought. He was scheduled to work tomorrow night, and the only other guy that would be able to cover for him was out of town. He started making phone calls to see who could be on watch tomorrow night. He wanted people there early on and wanted them there all night long, if needed. Unfortunately, only two people were available. And of the two, the only one who would commit to more than an hour was Jeremy. Okay, he'd have three, maybe four hours of coverage from the bench across the street from the Windsor Inn.

THIRTY-THREE

Annette sat there in tears after her date with Jeremy. Thoughts were whirling around in her head. Out of the clear blue she thought about a conversation she'd had with her parents when she was a teen, living at home. They talked about falling in love, but also about being involved with someone who you really liked and had things in common with. They said that sex was best with someone that you loved, and that when it happened, it would be great. For the first time, she understood this advice. It was advice that she didn't think about at the time, advice that went unheeded as she had gone about her own sexually charged agenda. And there she was at this juncture in her life. She felt she had met that person and she couldn't even kiss him.

It wasn't that late, so she decided to call Cindy on her cell phone.

Cindy answered and Annette said, "Hi, Cin, it's Annette. Is the doctor in?"

"Yeah, what's up, girl?"

"Can we talk?"

"Uh, yeah. Can I call you back or did you want to

meet?"

"Can I come over?"

"Sure, I'm in the middle of something, but I can wrap it up by the time you get here."

About twenty minutes later, Annette arrived at Cindy's apartment, and Cindy greeted her with open arms.

Cindy looked at Annette and said, "You look terrible, have you been crying?"

"Yes," Annette said, "I had a thing with Jeremy."

They sat down on Cindy's couch.

"What happened?"

"He took me out to eat."

"Oh, I hate when *that* happens."

"No, Cindy. He took me out on a date. He took me to the Italian place, Ristorante Con Brio."

"Oh, no. That's where you picked up that bartender." Cindy's eyes grew wide, and she put one hand over her own mouth. "Oh God! That's where you picked up the guy after my birthday dinner who smacked the shit out of you! What did you do?"

"I freaked. I totally freaked, and Jeremy has no clue why. It was terrible."

"I'm sorry, Annie."

"I don't know what to do or what to tell him. He deserves better than me."

"Bullshit! That's bullshit, Annie. There's no better than you unless being a virgin is better. You have committed no crime, sweetie. And it's not like you've cheated on him or anything. All that stuff happened before you guys met."

"I know. I know."

They both sat there for a moment looking at each other, Annette on the verge of tears. Cindy hated to see her that way.

"You know what you gotta do?" Cindy said.

"No."

"It's come to Jesus time, baby. You've got to talk to the man. I don't think he deserves better, but I think he deserves to know what's going on. I mean, it isn't necessarily any of his business, but I don't think you're ever gonna let it rest until you get it off your chest. You know?"

There was a moment of silence. Cindy continued, "I think you've gotta tell him about all of this stuff for your own sake. And then you can move on."

"But what if he freaks? What if he decides that he's not interested in me anymore?"

"I don't know. I don't think you can help that. But I don't think you want to go on like this, either."

They sat there on Cindy's couch, and Cindy wrapped her arms around Annette.

THIRTY-FOUR

It was a beautiful clear night, the night of a full moon, and Jeremy was sitting on the bench across from the Windsor Inn. He stood and walked out from under the awning, moving a little closer to the curb so he could see the moon. He stood there with his hands in his jacket pockets, staring up at the moon, lost in thought. Occasionally he looked over across the street at the Windsor, and then he'd glance up and down the street, but so far it had been a pretty quiet night without too much activity on the street. Every once in a while, he'd see people moving about, and he'd take a look, but so far he'd spied no one that looked remotely like the suspect he was watching for. He looked back up at the moon again, studying its features, and became lost in thought. He was in such a weird mood. He had such a mélange of feelings out there in the moonlight on this eerie night. He was more than a little nervous about the possibility of running into the guy, a guy with a history of violence. Tom had been pretty excited when he called to get Jeremy's help. Luckily, Jeremy didn't have a gig tonight, so he was able to help out. But Tom's revelation that their perpetrator had attacked all of his victims on the night of a full moon made it seem pretty likely that if they were finally going to spot this guy, it would be tonight.

Jeremy knew that if he identified the guy, he was supposed to call 911 first and then immediately call Tom, who was working down the street at The Applegate. But Jeremy had also considered the possibility that the guy would be on his way in with another woman and that neither the police nor Tom would arrive in time. He wasn't quite sure what he'd do in that case, but it seemed to him a likely scenario.

Jeremy had other things on his mind, too. He had been feeling so great, so alive, so in love. He thought that he probably shouldn't feel that strongly about Annette. He shouldn't be in love with her. They hadn't been going together that long, and he felt like he was just being too . . . optimistic, like he wasn't being realistic about the possibilities for his relationship with her. But he was crazy about her. He loved hanging out with her, loved the kind of person that she was, loved talking to her, and what really killed him was that she seemed to really like him. She seemed to really be turned on by him. It was such a unique, exhilarating time in his life—and then it all seemed to go wrong.

What happened that night? He wasn't quite sure if she was getting sick, or if there was something going on in her life that he didn't know about, or maybe she'd just decided, like the girl before, that she was done with him and didn't know how to break the bad news. All he knew was he thought they had something going on, and when he tried to kiss her, she turned her head. He was still staring up at the moon when he remembered the beautiful redhead that had come on to him and taken him into her bedroom. *God, what a night that was.* He couldn't believe she took all of her clothes off like that, and when he tried to kiss her, she turned her head. He just didn't get it.

He looked across the street and scanned up and down once again. Nothing. He finally turned around, stepped back over to the bench, and sat down. He'd told Tom he could stay for a couple of hours. *But what the hell,* he thought. *I might as well stay out here all night long. I've got nothing better to do*. He started feeling alone and lonely. His errant mind started to torment him again. *Still a virgin. You'll always be a virgin. Annette doesn't care about you. She's done with you.* He heard two car doors slam, and his mind snapped back. A car had just parked on the other side a little way up the street, not too far from the Windsor. *Oh God! That's him.* The suspect had just gotten out of the car and there was a young woman with him getting out on the other side. Jeremy grabbed the cell phone out of his pocket and hit 9ll.

"Nine-one-one, what is your emergency?"

"I need the police at the corner of Applegate and Pine right away," Jeremy responded in a hushed tone.

"We'll get someone out as soon as possible. What's happening?"

"I'm on a surveillance watch, and I just saw the suspect we've been looking for. He's going into the Windsor Inn with a young woman."

At about that time, Jeremy saw the doors of the Windsor close as they went in. He bolted into the street. The next thing he heard was the sound of screeching tires, and he looked up to see the grille of an oncoming bus. He put his hand up to the grille and danced backward there in the street with his one arm outstretched as the bus came to a stop just in time.

"Are you okay, sir?" the 911 operator asked.

"Yes, ma'am. Please notify Detective Saunders. He's on the case."

"Yes, sir, and can I have your name?"

"Jeremy Reynolds," and he put the cell phone in his pocket as he stepped in the door of the Windsor.

There was an older gentleman at the reception desk to his right. Jeremy looked down the hall with rows of doors on either side that stretched out in front of him but didn't see anybody. He heard the elevator door close.

"Excuse me, sir. Are there any stairs?"

The clerk at the desk pointed to an alcove a little farther down the hallway. Jeremy jogged down the hall, his heart still pounding from the near miss with the bus. He bolted up two flights of stairs to the second floor and then waited and listened before he opened the door to the upstairs hallway. He thought he heard the sound of a woman's laughter in the hall. He didn't want to just pop out and try to confront this guy, but he wanted to see which room they went into. He eased the door open and looked up the hallway just in time to see a door closing. He walked slowly, cautiously up the hallway. It was room 213. He walked back down the hallway and slipped into the stairwell so he could call Tom.

*

Tom had been checking his cell phone frequently, but had not received any word from Jeremy yet. He didn't ordinarily care about his cell phone when he was at his usual post at The Applegate, but he did tonight, and unfortunately the music was loud enough that he wasn't sure he'd be able to hear it, so he set it on vibrate mode. Tom, however, was in the middle of his own situation, which had started shortly before. The same guy he'd asked to leave once before was back and up to his usual misbehavior. It was the same guy that had harassed Annette some time ago. "Mr. Impolite" had been drinking way too much on this occasion and was pretty much making a nuisance of himself to more than one of the women there. Tom had been keeping an eye on him for a while even though no one had complained yet. Mr. Impolite had been standing at a particular table for the last several minutes, talking to a couple of young women, but he could tell by their demeanor and the looks on their faces that they were becoming annoyed.

When the guy accidentally knocked over one of the drinks on the table, spilling it everywhere, Tom just walked up and said, "Sir, you've got to leave." He then looked over at the young woman who was trying to clean up her lap with a napkin and said, "I'm sorry, ma'am. We'll get you another drink on the house."

Mr. Impolite was still standing there ignoring Tom. Tom repeated himself, "Sir, you've got to leave. Now."

"Says who?" Mr. Impolite responded.

"Says me," Tom responded in his usual calm voice.

"Well, it's a free fuckin' country, and I'll leave when I'm ready."

Tom rolled his eyes. He held up his hands with his palms facing out and said, "Sir, I don't want to have any problems. Please, you've got to leave."

The guy wobbled backward one step and caught his balance. "Well, you can't make me, asshole!"

At that moment, the buzzer on Tom's phone went off. He grabbed the guy by one wrist, flipped him around, took the guy's other arm, forced it up behind his back, and marched him toward the door. One of the bartenders held the door open, and Tom pushed the guy out the door onto the sidewalk. It happened so fast, the guy didn't know what was happening. Tom literally had the guy out of the door by the time his buzzer went off a third time.

He looked at the bartender and said, "Don't let that fool back in here."

He snatched the cell phone out of his pocket and saw that it was Jeremy calling, but it was too late. Jeremy had already hung up.

*

Jeremy heard the sound of a woman scream. He jammed the phone in his pocket, jumped out of the stairwell, and ran down the hall to room 213. He froze in front of the door for a moment and then heard what sounded like someone being hit. The woman screamed again from behind that door. He pounded on the door. There was silence for a few moments.

He pounded on the door again, and a male voice from behind the door said, "Who is it?"

"Uh, it's the neighborhood watch!" Jeremy shouted.

At that moment, the door opened, and he was face-to-face with the man in the sketch.

"Who the fuck are you?"

"I'm with the neighborhood watch. The police are on their way."

He grabbed Jeremy by his shirt and pulled him into the room. The woman was naked on the bed. Her face was bleeding. Gerald Swan figured if this guy was trying to protect this slut then he was no better than her.

"Are you trying to protect this slut?" he hollered, and then he punched Jeremy in the face.

Jeremy tried to return a blow, but Swan hit him a

second time in quick succession and knocked Jeremy off his feet. The young woman was sitting on the bed with her knees pulled up to her chest, screaming in horror. Swan kneeled down astride Jeremy and pounded him again several times as blood flew. The woman scooted off the end of the bed and tried to run out of the room, but Swan leaped up and threw her back down on the bed. Jeremy lay there on the floor next to the bed with blood running down his face, unconscious, when the door flew open. Tom burst in and threw Swan onto the floor. He immediately tried to get back up, but Tom just knocked him onto his back again. Tom already had his cell phone out.

"Don't get up," he said, and a voice came over Tom's cell phone. "Nine-one-one. What's your emergency?"

"Police and ambulance to the Windsor Inn, Applegate and Pine."

Swan yelled up at Tom. "Don't mess with me, big man! I'm a karate expert."

Tom replied, "Uh huh," and continued his conversation with the 911 operator.

Swan jumped back up with rage in his eyes and, without even looking at Swan, Tom kicked his legs out from under him so fast, Swan never knew what happened.

Tom said, "Excuse me," to the 911 operator.

Swan was back on the floor, wincing from the pain of the last fall. Tom finally looked Swan in the eye, extended his arm down toward him with his index finger pointed up, and said in a very slow, deliberate voice, "I said. Don't. Get. Up."

The sound of sirens echoed from the street, and Tom saw the blue lights of police cars flashing through the window of the room.

Moments later, the police came in. An ambulance arrived some minutes after that to take Jeremy and the young woman to the hospital.

THIRTY-FIVE

Jeremy's eyes flew open to the sound of a siren. He was on his back, and there was something pressed over his nose and mouth. He was on a gurney in an ambulance on his way to the emergency room. A young man with a crew cut smiled down at him and lifted the oxygen mask off of his face.

The paramedic said, "Well, glad you could join us."

Jeremy just blinked up at him, immediately aware of great pain in his face.

"What's your name?" the paramedic asked.

"Jeremy."

"Last name?"

"Reynolds."

"Do you know today's date?"

"No."

"What about the day of the week?"

"It's Friday night. And it's a full moon."

"Alright, and how old are you?"

"Twenty-two."

"Okay, Jeremy. We're on our way to the emergency room. We'll be there soon. Is there anyone you'd like to contact?"

"Yeah, I guess we should call my mom."

When they arrived and wheeled him in through the sliding glass doors, Tom jogged in the door just behind them. "Jeremy, glad you're awake, man. I am so sorry. I got your call and came straight away."

Jeremy responded, "Did you get the guy?"

"Yes, we did. Yes, we did! I'm going to help you get checked in here, and then I gotta get over to the police station. You're my hero, man."

They wheeled Jeremy directly into an examination area, and a doctor came in a few minutes later.

*

Arlene Reynolds was sleeping soundly when the phone on her bedside table rang. Her eyes flew open and she looked over at the clock. It was shortly after midnight. She turned on the lamp and picked up the receiver of the phone.

"Hello?"

"Yes, is this Ms. Reynolds?"

"Yes, it is."

"Hi, Ms. Reynolds, I'm sorry to bother you. My name is Tom Garrison, and I'm calling for your son, Jeremy."

"Oh my God! What's happened?"

"He's okay, Ms. Reynolds. I think he's going to be fine, but there's been a situation. He's in the emergency room at the hospital near the school."

"Oh, I was afraid something like this would happen. Was this about that surveillance . . . watch thing he was doing?"

"Yes, ma'am. He spotted the suspect and intervened before I or the police could get there. He took a few blows to the head." Tom thought he could hear Ms. Reynolds crying at that point. "I'm very sorry, ma'am. I never wanted anyone to get hurt."

"No, no, I don't blame you. What happened to the guy you were looking for?"

"The police have him in custody."

"Okay then. I'm on my way. It'll take me at least an hour, but I'm on my way."

"I'll let Jeremy know you're coming."

*

After he finished the call with Jeremy's mother, Tom spoke with the receptionist and then left for the police station. It was a couple of hours before the dust finally settled, but Tom had another thought. He was aware of the budding romance between Jeremy and Annette and thought that he should give her a call even though it was the middle of the night.

When Annette answered, Tom said, "Annette, this is Tom. We've had a situation. Jeremy was on watch duty at the Windsor—"

"Jeremy?" she interjected.

"Yes, Jeremy Reynolds."

"I didn't know he was involved."

"Well, he doesn't look too good right now. I'm at the police station, but I'm going back over as soon as I can. He's in the ER."

"I'm on my way."

*

Not long after, the doors of the emergency room slid open, and Annette strode up to the admittance counter and asked, "Is Jeremy Reynolds here?"

The woman behind the counter relayed that he was, but that he had been taken to radiology for testing.

"Have a seat in the waiting room. I'll let you know when he's back."

Annette looked around, but didn't see Tom. There were a number of people in the waiting area, but one person caught her attention. It was a woman who looked to be in her forties with curly, medium-length blond hair who was looking right at her. Something about the woman's eyes told Annette who she was.

"Do you know Jeremy?" the woman inquired as soon as Annette walked up.

Annette sat down beside her. "Yes, my name is Annette."

They immediately, instinctively, reached out for each

other with both hands.

Turning toward each other in their seats, clutching each other's hands, Arlene spoke, "I'm Jeremy's mom," and she began to cry very softly.

They just sat for a moment, feeling each other's compassion and concern for Jeremy, feeling the worry that they both carried for a loved one that they shared in this surreal moment, having never met before.

Arlene finally spoke. "I saw Jeremy when I got here, before they took him back to get a CT scan. Oh God." She paused. "He looks pretty bad."

She paused for another moment to collect herself. At this point, Annette had one hand over her mouth as she looked into Jeremy's mother's face and listened.

Arlene continued. "They're scanning his head to make sure he doesn't have any internal bleeding or anything."

"I just got a call from Tom a little while ago," Annette said. "He was at the police station. I didn't even know Jeremy was involved in this until Tom told me just tonight."

"Jeremy speaks very fondly of you."

Arlene paused before speaking again, obviously not quite knowing how to ask what was on her mind. But Annette already knew the question.

"I was one of the girls," Annette said.

"Oh, honey." They reached for each other and held each other. Jeremy's mom held the back of Annette's head softly as they relaxed their embrace and said, "What a terrible thing. No one deserves that."

Annette began to weep, releasing herself, forgiving herself in that moment. She cried out inside of herself, wanting to confess, needing to confess her sins to this woman, to this woman who she had only just met. "I've been such a terrible person, Ms. Reynolds."

"Oh, honey."

"I mean, before I met Jeremy I was . . . I mean I was just such a terrible person," she whispered through her tears.

"What was so terrible?" Arlene said softly, and she just let the question hang in the air for Annette.

"I used to . . . I used to see a lot of guys . . . I mean, I used to pick up guys just because I wanted to have sex with them."

Arlene sat expressionless, and suddenly Annette felt completely out of control emotionally. She lost all connection in that moment with Jeremy's mother, not knowing what this woman was thinking or feeling or what she may have thought about her.

But Arlene did not respond. She did not pass judgment. She did not forgive. She did not condone. And this void took the air out of the room as Annette was left with nothing, with no one but herself.

THIRTY-SIX

Tom was exhausted. He was emotionally drained and ragged. It had been a very long day that culminated in another innocent person being beaten unconscious. His day had started early in the morning before the trauma of that moonlit Friday night. By eight o'clock that morning, he had started his own martial arts practice at home, which lasted about an hour and a half. Then it was off to a mid-morning class at the community college. He had just enough time after that to stop into the cafeteria, grab a bite to eat, and make a few phone calls. He was just double-checking to make sure everyone he had lined up would be on their post that evening across from the Windsor Inn. After he finished lunch, he got into his car and drove to the *dojang* where he instructed martial arts classes. He made it just in time to park his car, run in, get changed, and teach the class. After class, he took time, as was his practice, to answer questions and talk with any of the students who approached him. He then touched base by phone with Savannah, took a quick shower, put on some fresh clothes, and then it was off to work at The Applegate. That was just the start, it seemed.

It had been a crazy night at The Applegate. That would have been no big deal, but he was on edge the whole night, wondering when his cell phone would go off, knowing that his volunteers on lookout down the street were very much at risk. He was cool, in control. When he got the phone call from Jeremy, he exploded into action. When he burst through the door of room 213 at the Windsor and saw Jeremy lying there on the floor bleeding, he kept his cool, stayed in control, and handled the situation. Then he went to the emergency room. And he stayed cool, in control, when he called Jeremy's mother. Then he went to the police station and spent hours with Detective Saunders. And he was cool, in control, when he finally walked back through the sliding doors of the emergency room at the hospital. The sight of Jeremy lying on the motel room floor unconscious and bleeding was lodged in his heart the moment he first saw it. But he had stayed cool and in control until this moment when he walked into the waiting area and saw Annette with Jeremy's mother.

Annette had been sitting there in front of Ms. Reynolds, suspended, when she felt the new presence as Tom came into the waiting area. She immediately stood, ran up to him, and delicately put her arms around his huge frame as he lowered his head and began to gently weep. She rubbed him on the back. All of the stress and emotion that he had kept in check was now overflowing. As Tom had held and steadied Annette the night that she had been beaten by Gerald Swan, so she now held and steadied Tom on this night.

After a few moments of respite, he leaned down and extended his hand to Jeremy's mother saying, "Ms. Reynolds?"

"Yes."

"Hello, Ms. Reynolds, I'm Tom Garrison. I'm sorry I wasn't here when you arrived. I've been at the police station."

"No, no, not at all. Please, call me Arlene."

"Have you seen Jeremy?"

"Yes, but they've taken him back to get a CT scan, and then they're going to set him up in a room."

At about that time, the doctor walked into the waiting area to speak with Ms. Reynolds.

"Well, good news," he said. "The CT scan didn't show any internal bleeding, and no fractures in his face or his head. Looks like he's going to be okay outside of some cuts and severe bruising."

At that moment, the air seemed to come back into the room, and everyone was able to breathe.

The doctor continued. "We're going to admit him just to be on the safe side and monitor him for a few hours. We'll probably kick him loose a little later today, maybe around noon time."

The doctor dismissed himself as everyone thanked him. A short time later, one of the staff came into the waiting area to let them know what room Jeremy was in. They all went up together and filed into his room. His face was pretty well bandaged up, but he offered a certain smile when they all came in. Jeremy's mother, Tom, and Annette were all relieved to see Jeremy and to know that he was going to be okay. Within a few minutes, Jeremy was asleep.

Tom expressed his relief that Jeremy was going to be alright and offered his condolences for Jeremy's injuries to Arlene. She was gracious and appreciative not only of Tom's concern, but of his efforts to catch the man who had beaten so many young women.

"Thank you, Arlene," Tom said. "Annette, Detective Saunders will be contacting you tomorrow—well, actually later today, I guess. They'll be having a lineup so you can identify the suspect."

It never occurred to Tom that this might be a sensitive topic to discuss in Jeremy's mother's presence, but at that point it didn't matter.

"Okay. Goodnight," Tom said, and with that he waved and left the room.

Arlene and Annette sat on either side of the room as Jeremy slept.

Arlene finally spoke and said softly to Annette, "You're a brave young woman."

THIRTY-SEVEN

It was mid-morning, and Gerald was away on one of his business trips when her cell phone rang.

"Hello, Mrs. Swan?"

"Yes."

"Hi, my name is David Kincade. I'm an attorney calling on behalf of your husband."

"Is something the matter?" she questioned.

"Yes, I'm afraid Mr. Swan has been arrested. I'm in the process of getting him released on bond."

"What happened? What was he arrested for?"

"I can explain everything when you get here, Mrs. Swan. We're at the third precinct on Cockade Street. But we're going to need to use a property bond which will require your signature."

She paused. With a sense of enthusiasm and a faint smile she decided and said, "I'll be there shortly."

When Betty walked into the police station, a gentleman in a dark suit approached her from the waiting area near the front desk.

"Hello, Mrs. Swan?" he inquired.

"Yes," she said.

"Hi, I'm David Kincade. I'm representing your husband, Gerald. Thanks for coming down as quickly as you have. I promise you we'll get him out of here just as quickly as possible."

She paused, looked at him, and said, "Not if I can help it." Then she turned her back to face the officer at the front desk. "I'd like to report a crime. I'd like to report my husband, Gerald Swan."

The officer responded, "What did he do, ma'am?"

With the determination of cold steel, she said, "Look at my face. He did this to me last week."

The officer looked at her and said, "Let me get Detective Saunders."

THIRTY-EIGHT

Later that day, Jeremy was released from the hospital. Despite her best efforts, Jeremy's mother couldn't talk him into moving back home for a few days. She relented and drove Jeremy home to his rooming house. She stayed with him for a few hours and went out to get them both something to eat later that afternoon. They sat together in his room and chitchatted over sandwiches she had picked up from the nearby coffee shop.

About the time Jeremy had been released from the hospital, Annette got the call from Detective Saunders and went to the police station to identify the suspect. She walked into the station, identified herself at the front desk, and asked for Detective Saunders. The officer thanked her and motioned for her to take a seat. Her stomach had butterflies as she waited. It had been a stressful and emotional time for her. Not to mention she had pretty much been up all night. She wasn't so much nervous about identifying the suspect as she was about her interaction with Jeremy's mom and about her relationship with Jeremy. She was still thinking about what Cindy had told her and remembered her words, "*It's come to Jesus time, baby. You've got to talk to the man." Jesus,* she thought, *I've already pretty much spilled the beans to his mom.* At about that time, Detective Saunders appeared and introduced himself. He walked her to the elevator. They rode together to the third floor, and he thanked her for coming forward and thanked her for coming to the lineup.

They went into an office for questioning as Detective Saunders filled out the paperwork. When they wrapped that up, he took her into a dimly lit room with a large window facing into another room. He introduced her to several of the other officers who were present and then directed one of them to "get the contestants." Detective Saunders assured her that no one in the other room would be able to see her and that they had already been through this process once before earlier that day with a different victim trying to identify the same suspect with the exact same group of men in the lineup. They waited and soon a door in the other room opened and five men walked in. All of them were almost identical in height and all of them had the same clothes on. She was surprised that they could find so many people that looked so much alike and began to get nervous. But then she saw his face. She took one look at his face and knew. She took another look at his hands, which appeared quite large compared to everybody else's, and that confirmed it.

"That's him. The third guy from the left," she said.

Saunders admonished her to take her time and look at

all of them. She took another quick look at all of their faces.

"I have," she said. "That's him."

"Gerald Swan," he replied.

He smiled and knocked on the glass.

When she left the police station, she headed straight over to Jeremy's. She was going to talk to him. She was just going to spill it and whatever happened would happen. She had a new sense of self and resigned herself to the possibility that Jeremy might be pretty well knocked off balance by her past. But she had already decided that she was going to be who she wanted to be, and that she would not be defined by her past.

Annette ran into Arlene just as she was coming down the front stairs of Jeremy's rooming house to leave for home.

They embraced, and as they stood there on the walkway, Ms. Reynolds said to Annette, "You know, I don't know exactly what the nature of your relationship with Jeremy is right now. It isn't necessarily any of my business as long as Jeremy is happy. But . . ." she paused, looked Annette in the eye, and continued, "spend some time. Get to know each other."

"Thank you, Ms. Reynolds," Annette responded.

She stood there for a moment after Arlene left, and the words rang so true in Annette's ears. It was the same advice her parents had tried to give her years ago.

She walked up the stairs of the rooming house, down

the hall to Jeremy's room and knocked.

"Hello?" she heard him say from the other side of the door.

"It's Annette," she responded. He opened the door and they just stood for a moment, neither of them quite sure how to respond.

"You look terrible," she finally said.

"Yeah, that's kind of what I thought. That's why I put all these bandages on. Some people wear hats. I'm wearing bandages."

"It's quite a fashion statement. Do they make those for women as well, then?"

"Yeah, they do. We'll have to go shopping together."

They were both enjoying the repartee.

"Hey, do you mind if I come in?"

"Please do," he said.

"I've got an apology to make to you."

They sat down, she on the chair and he on the edge of his bed.

She continued. "I know I was acting really strange the night you took me out to Ristorante Con Brio. I had been there before."

He just sat looking at her as she spoke. She took a moment to collect her thoughts.

"You know, I had no idea that you were part of Tom's watch team. Anyway, I was one of the girls that Swan beat up."

Jeremy's eyes were wide now with surprise.

"I had no idea," he said.

She continued. "Well, first I want to thank you for helping Tom, and helping to get this guy, but there's more to the story." She hesitated and then the words came tumbling out. "I picked that guy up. I was at Con Brio, and I thought he was good-looking, and I wanted to have sex with somebody, and I seduced him."

Jeremy sat there, expressionless.

"He called me a slut. I tried to leave and he hit me, threw me down. Then he made me suck him, and he came in my mouth. And lots of guys have come in my mouth before, but only when I wanted them to, and nobody ever called me a slut before."

He just looked at her with his eyebrows pulled down, his face questioning, not knowing what to think or how to respond.

She continued. "I've been . . . I've been very promiscuous. Until that happened! And then I met you! I haven't had sex or anything with anybody for months now, Jeremy, and I don't care. But then I met you. I like you. I mean, it's all different now."

Her mind was spinning—spinning out of control because she really wanted him to understand. She wanted him to understand that she really liked him and that her relationship with him was so different from anything that she'd ever experienced, and so great. She started to sob, and she put her face in her hands.

"I wanted to kiss you," she said with her face still in her

hands. She sat there in tears, not knowing what to do or what to say next. She just waited in silence. Waited for the longest time.

Jeremy finally spoke in a very soft tone. "You know what's really funny?" He paused. "I'm a virgin."

Annette just sat there with her face in her hands as the words finally came through her emotional fog. She slowly lifted her head and looked at his face. They both looked at each other, trying to read the other's expression. He reached out his hand. Her jaw dropped and her eyes grew wide as she grabbed his hand, and they burst out howling in laughter.